JAKE MADDOX
GRAPHIC NOVELS

SOCCER SUPERSTAR

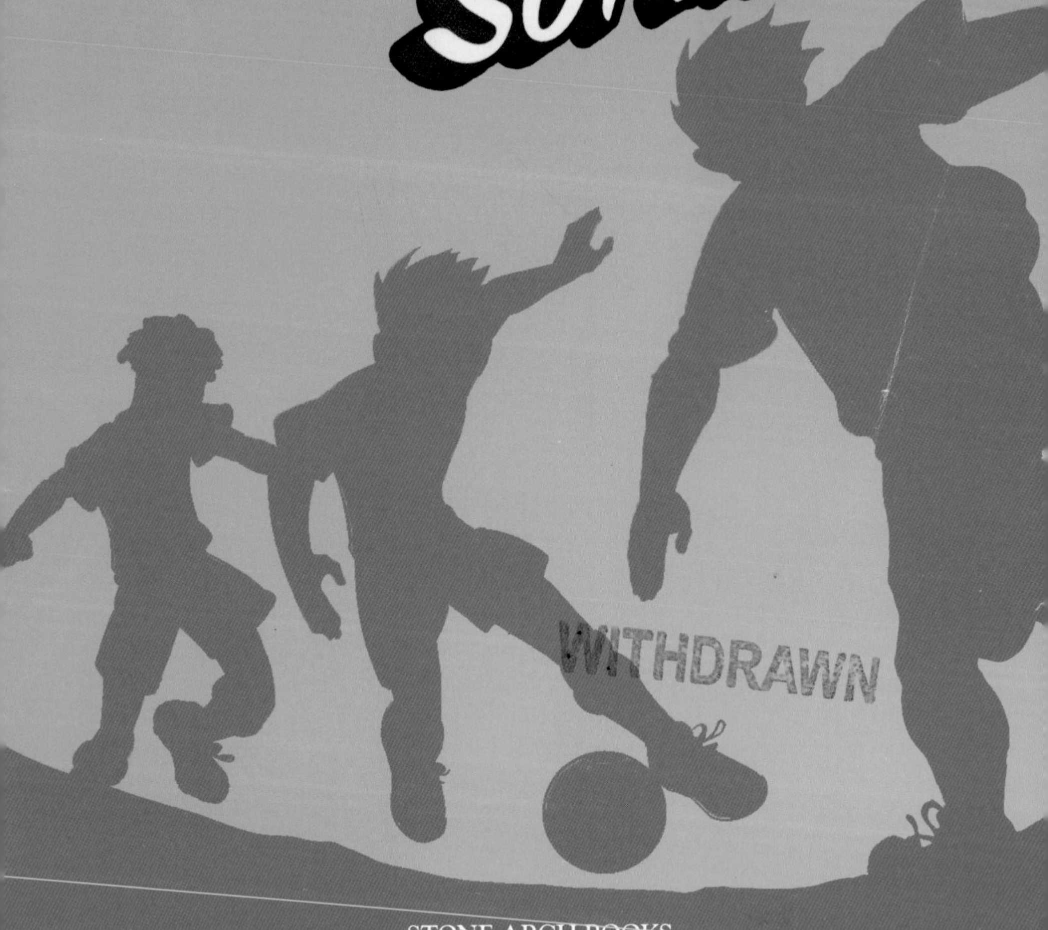

STONE ARCH BOOKS
a capstone imprint

JAKE MADDOX
GRAPHIC NOVELS

Published by Stone Arch Books,
an imprint of Capstone.
1710 Roe Crest Drive
North Mankato, Minnesota 56003
www.capstonepub.com

Library of Congress Cataloging-in-Publication Data
is available on the Library of Congress website.

ISBN: 978-1-4965-8378-9 (library binding)
ISBN: 978-1-4965-8457-1 (paperback)
ISBN: 978-1-4965-8383-3 (ebook PDF)

Summary: New kid Javier Moreno makes a big
splash on the soccer field when a video of his
amazing goal goes viral. But now the fame is going
to his head and he's hogging the ball and showing
off. Will Javi's solo act ruin the team's chances at
making the state championship?

Designed by Brann Garvey

Printed in the United States of America.
PA100

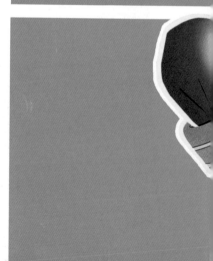

SOCCER SUPERSTAR

Text by Brandon Terrell
Art by Mel Joy San Juan
Lettering by Jaymes Reed
Cover Art by Berenice Muñiz

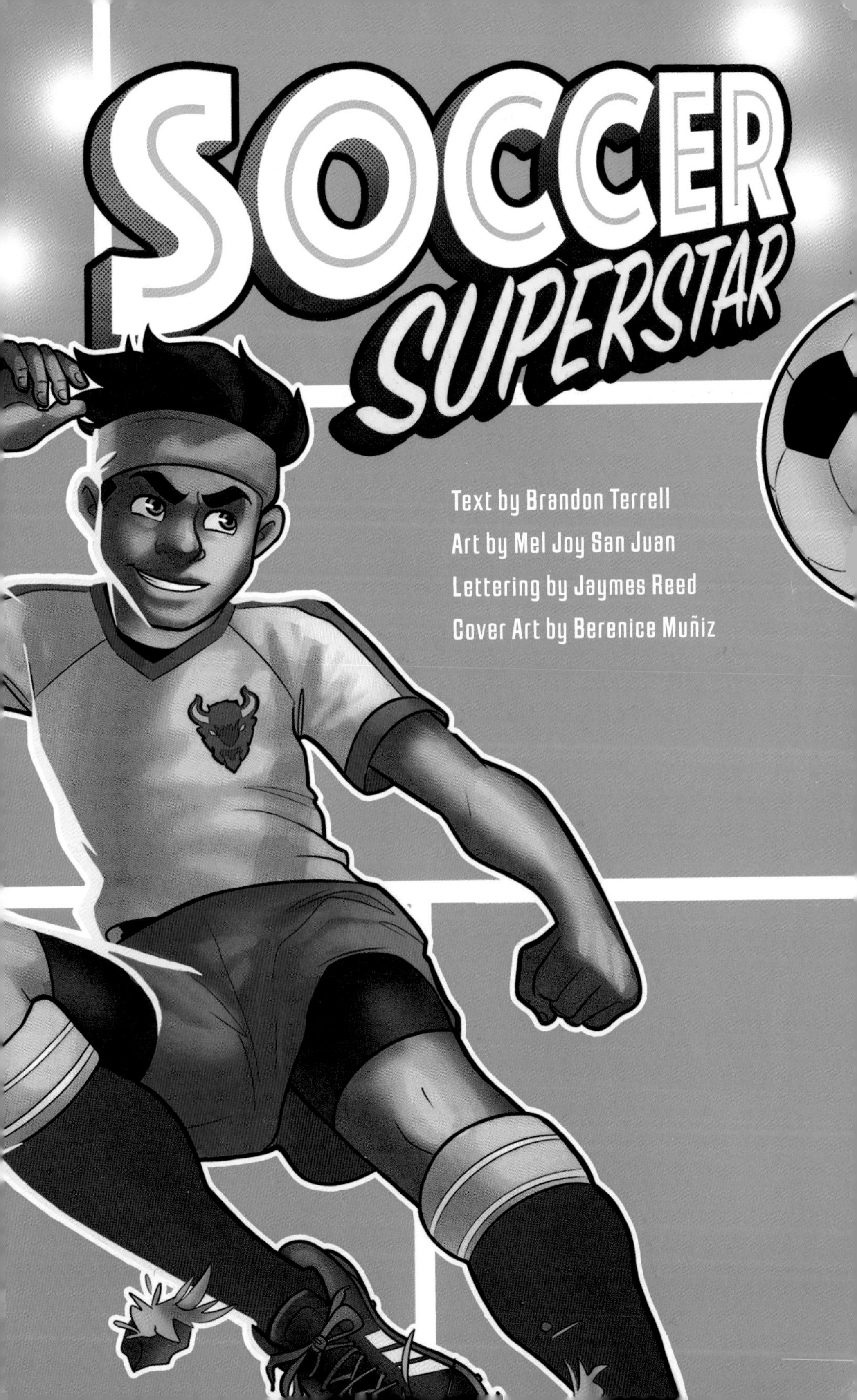

STARTING LINEUP

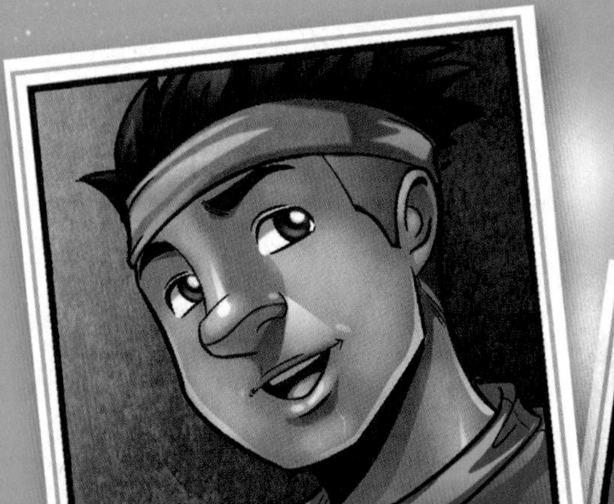
JAVIER MORENO

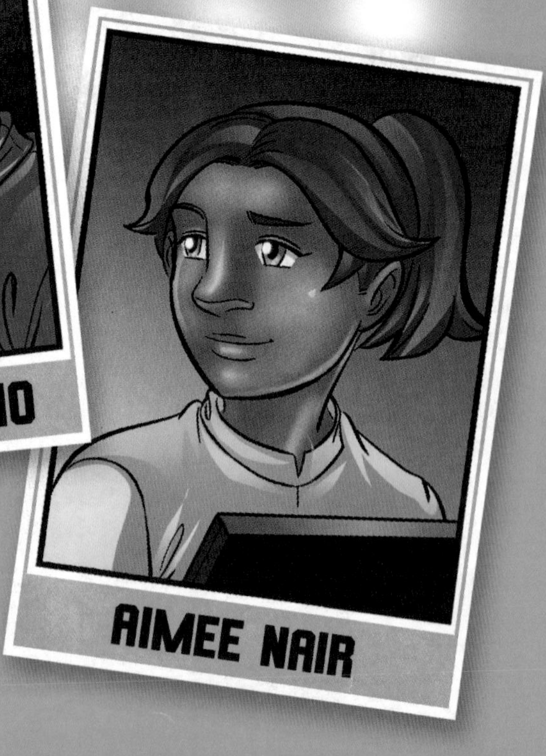
AIMEE NAIR

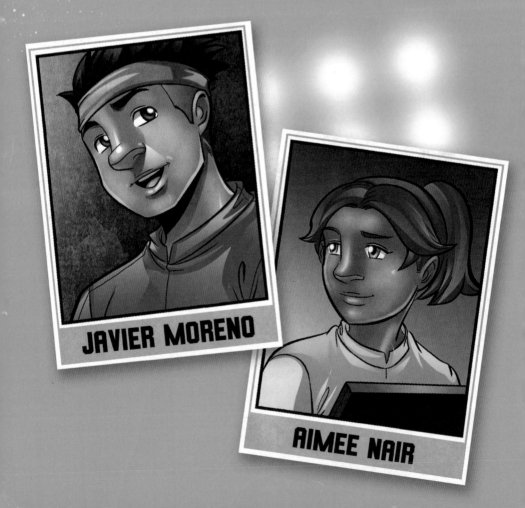

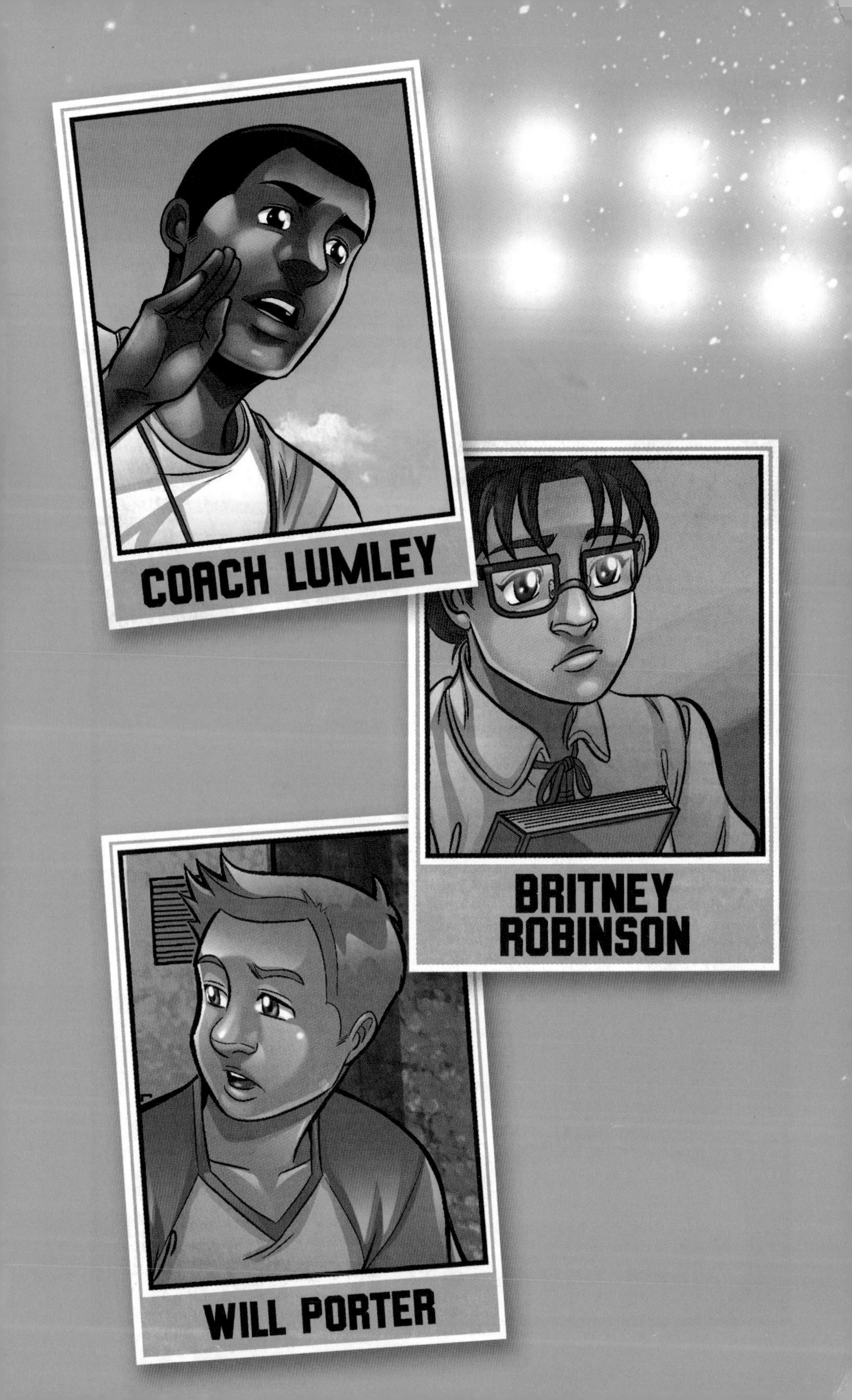
COACH LUMLEY
BRITNEY ROBINSON
WILL PORTER

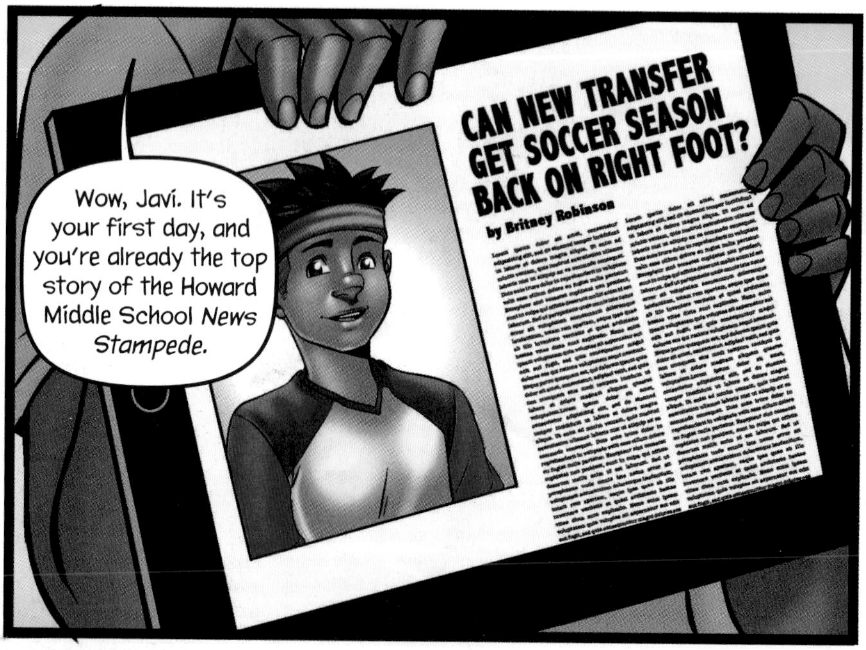
Wow, Javi. It's your first day, and you're already the top story of the Howard Middle School *News Stampede.*
CAN NEW TRANSFER GET SOCCER SEASON BACK ON RIGHT FOOT?
by Britney Robinson

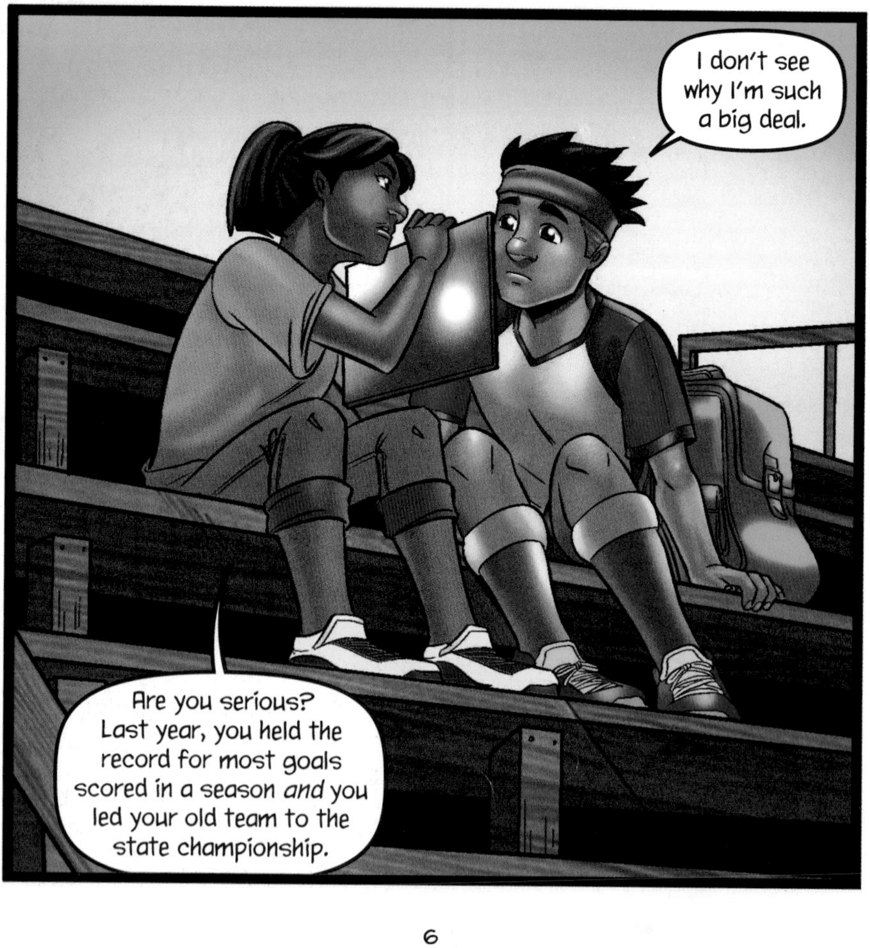
I don't see why I'm such a big deal.
Are you serious? Last year, you held the record for most goals scored in a season *and* you led your old team to the state championship.

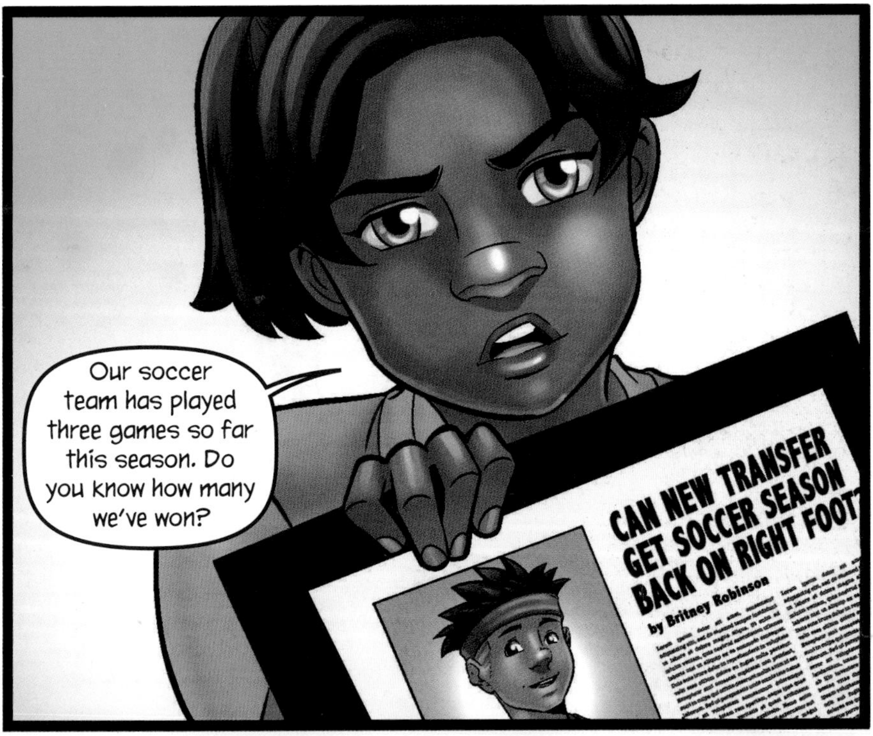
Our soccer team has played three games so far this season. Do you know how many we've won?
CAN NEW TRANSFER GET SOCCER SEASON BACK ON RIGHT FOOT?
by Britney Robinson

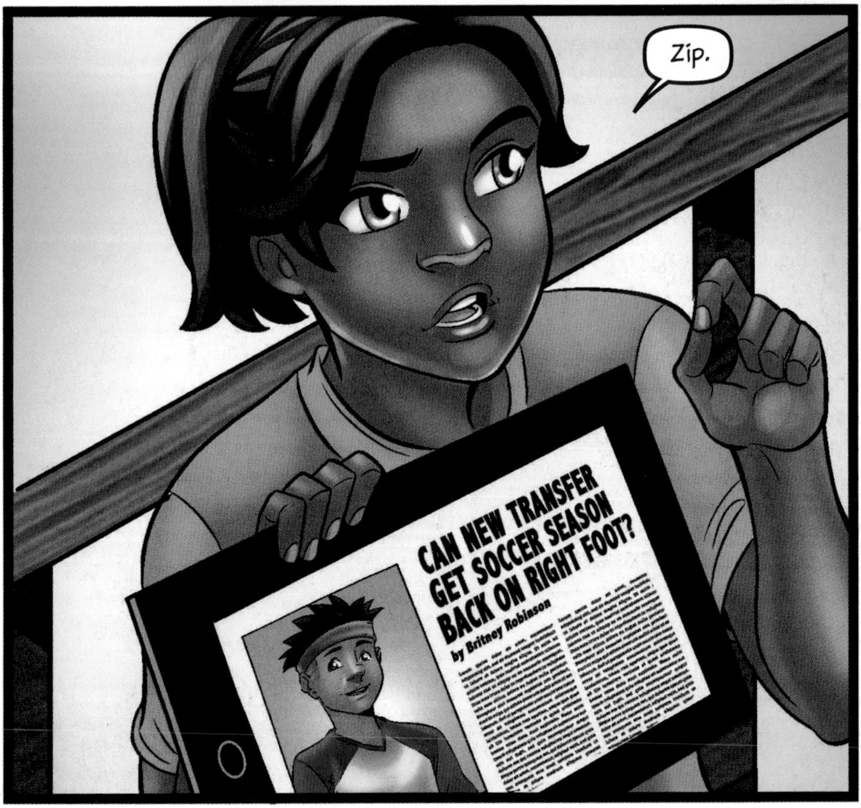
Zip.
CAN NEW TRANSFER GET SOCCER SEASON BACK ON RIGHT FOOT?
by Britney Robinson

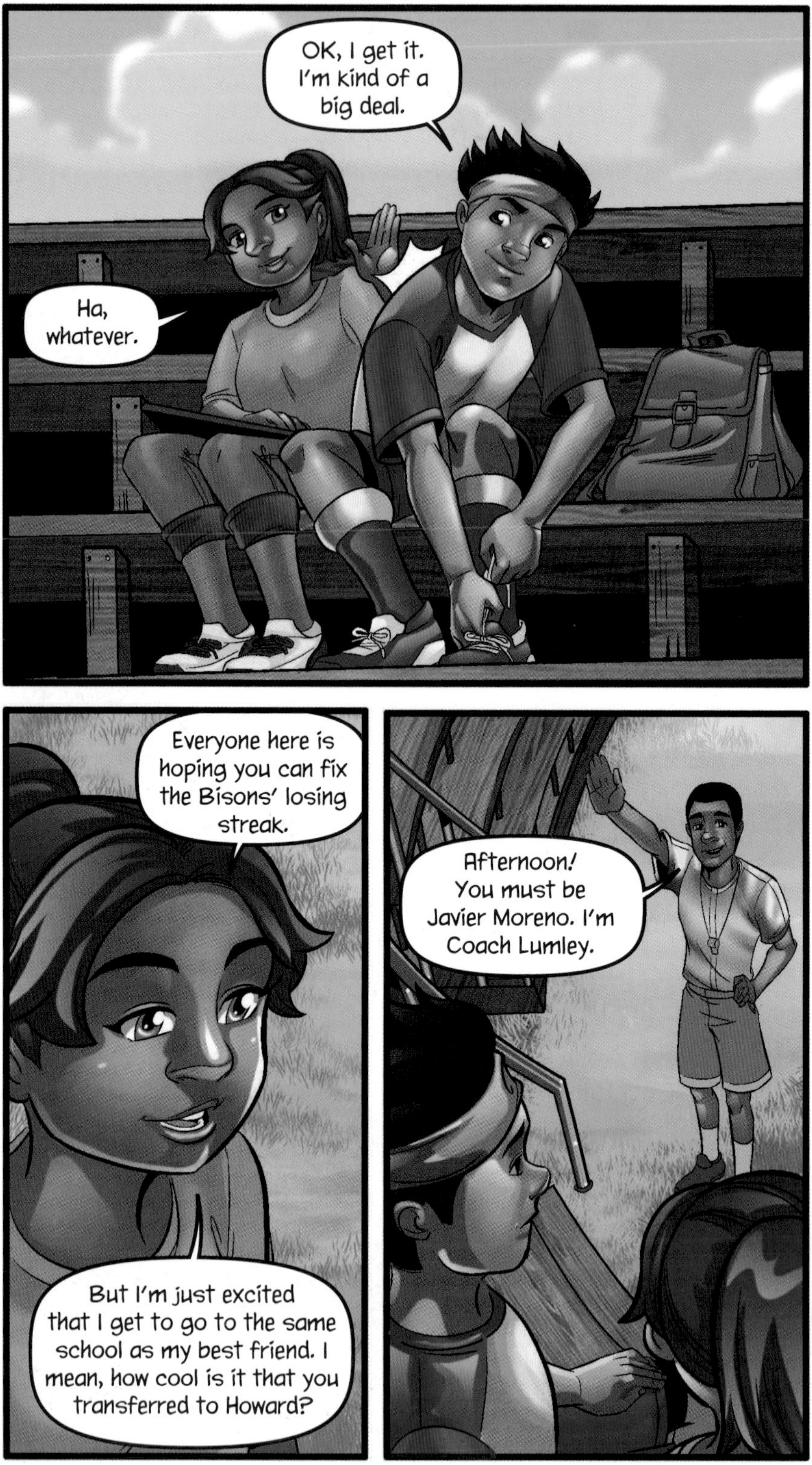
OK, I get it. I'm kind of a big deal.
Ha, whatever.
Everyone here is hoping you can fix the Bisons' losing streak.
But I'm just excited that I get to go to the same school as my best friend. I mean, how cool is it that you transferred to Howard?
Afternoon! You must be Javier Moreno. I'm Coach Lumley.

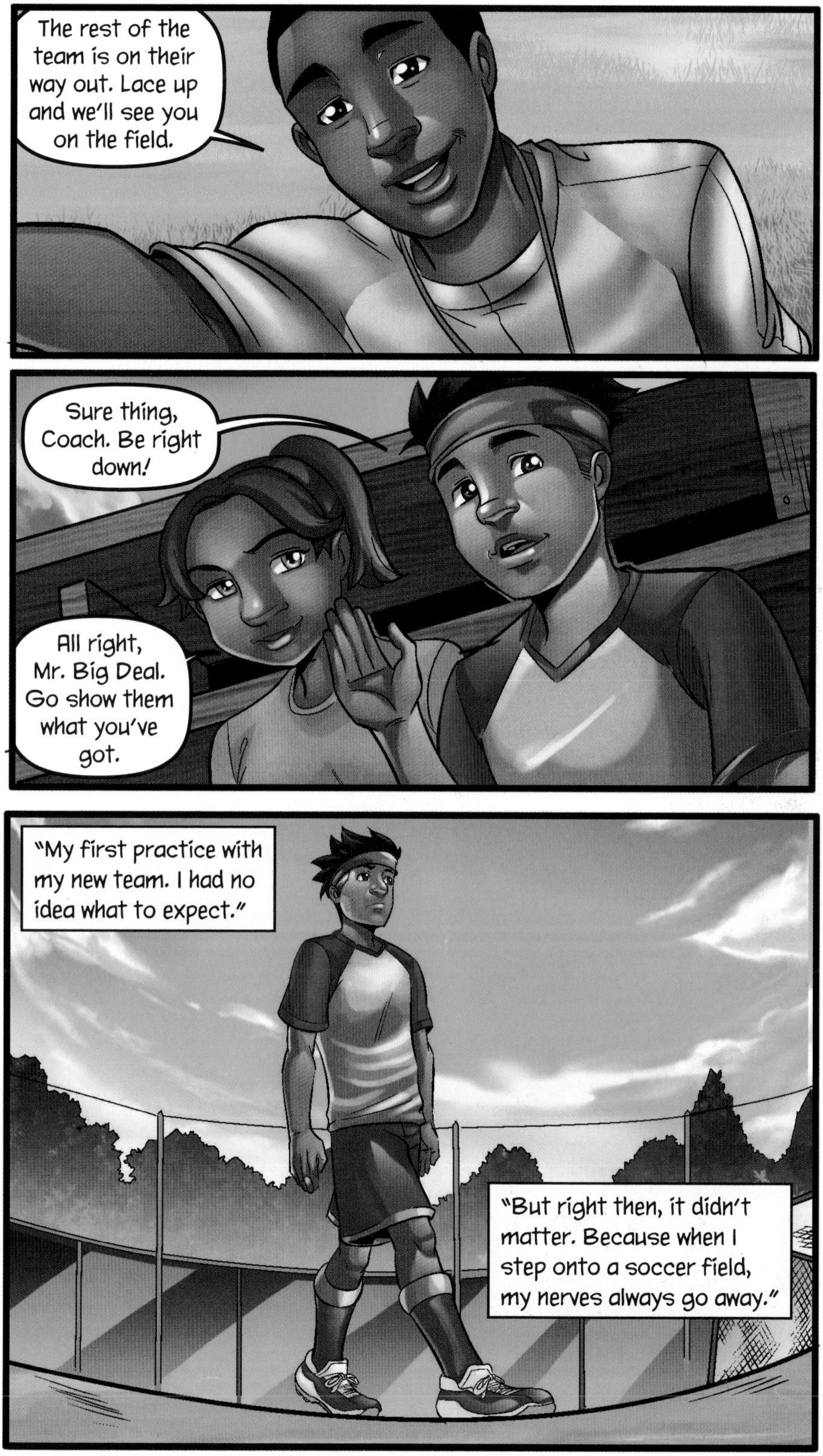
The rest of the team is on their way out. Lace up and we'll see you on the field.
Sure thing, Coach. Be right down!
All right, Mr. Big Deal. Go show them what you've got.
"My first practice with my new team. I had no idea what to expect."
"But right then, it didn't matter. Because when I step onto a soccer field, my nerves always go away."

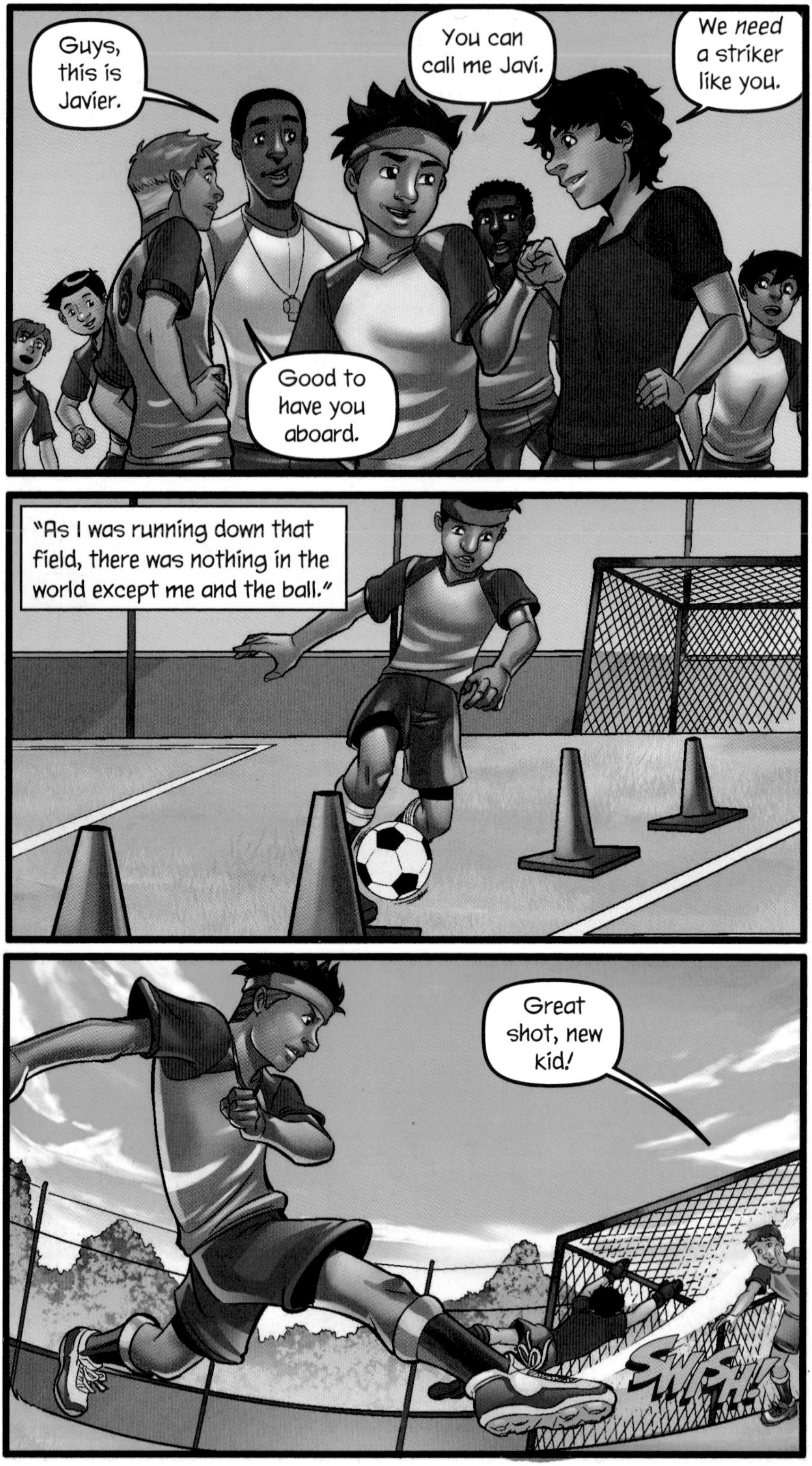
Guys, this is Javier.
You can call me Javi.
We *need* a striker like you.
Good to have you aboard.
"As I was running down that field, there was nothing in the world except me and the ball."
Great shot, new kid!
SWISH!

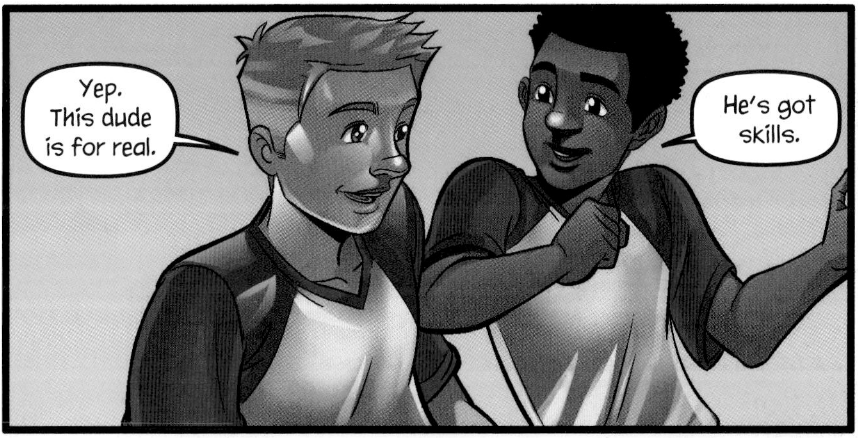
Yep. This dude is for real.
He's got skills.

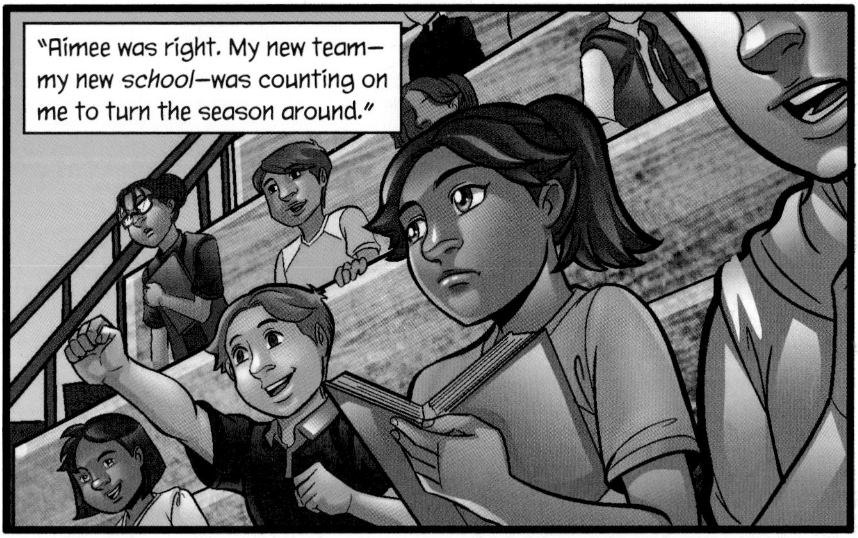
"Aimee was right. My new team—my new *school*—was counting on me to turn the season around."

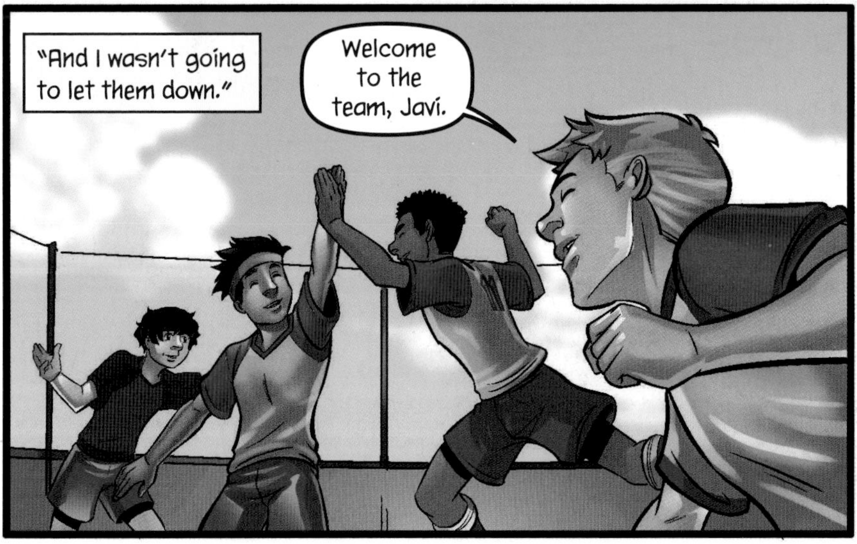
"And I wasn't going to let them down."
Welcome to the team, Javi.

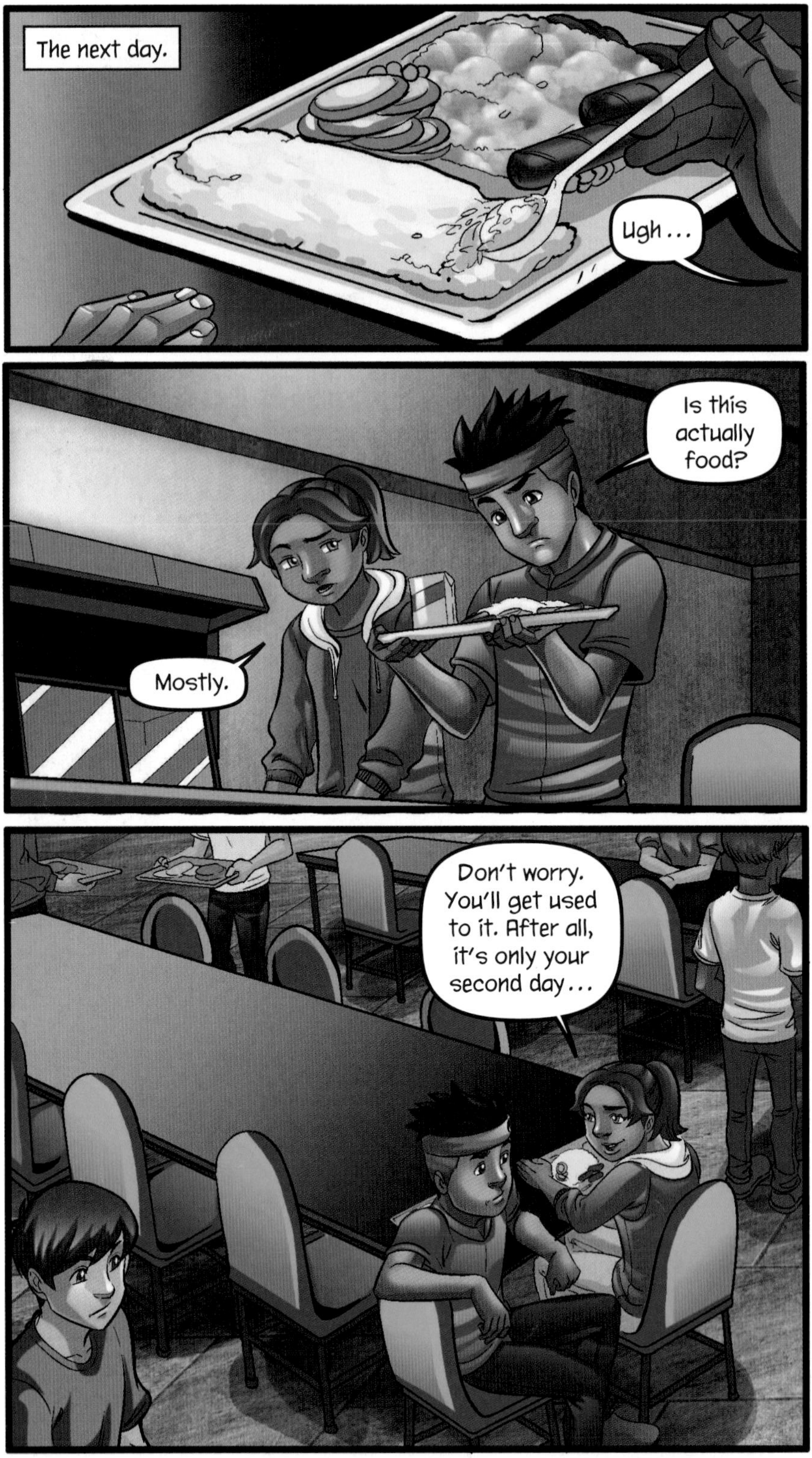
The next day.
Ugh . . .
Is this actually food?
Mostly.
Don't worry. You'll get used to it. After all, it's only your second day . . .

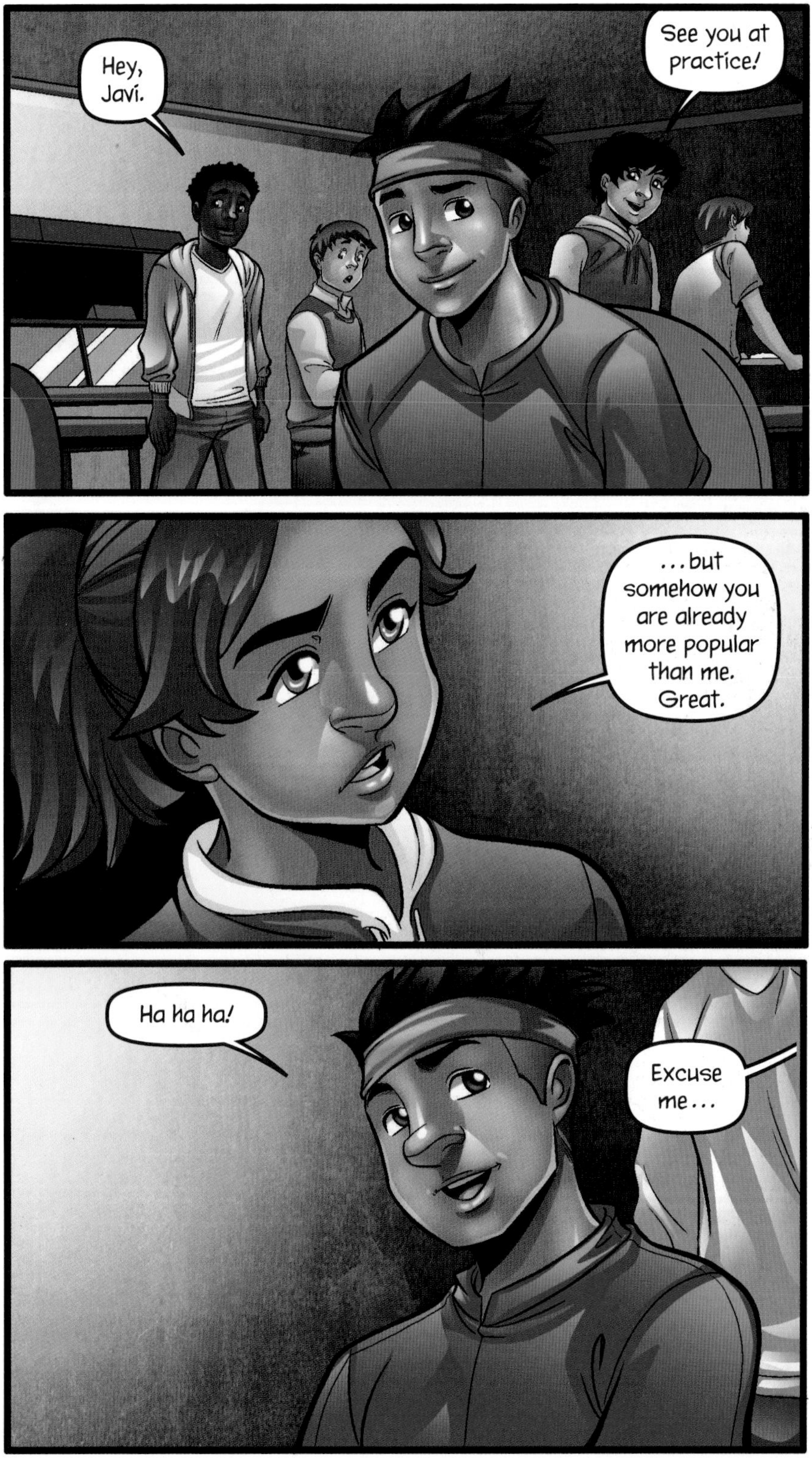
Hey, Javi.
See you at practice!
...but somehow you are already more popular than me. Great.
Ha ha ha!
Excuse me...

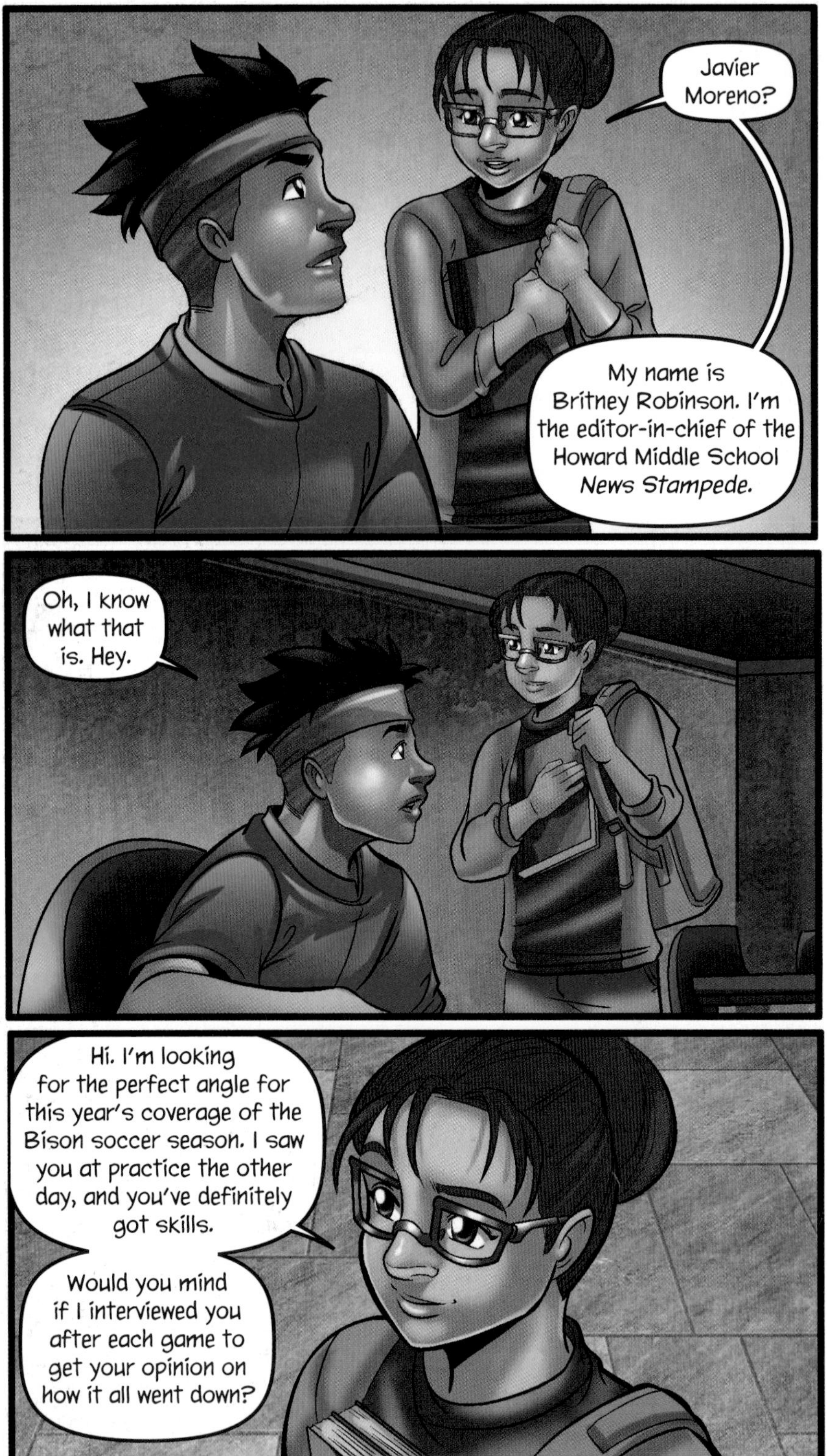
Javier Moreno?
My name is Britney Robinson. I'm the editor-in-chief of the Howard Middle School *News Stampede.*
Oh, I know what that is. Hey.
Hi. I'm looking for the perfect angle for this year's coverage of the Bison soccer season. I saw you at practice the other day, and you've definitely got skills.
Would you mind if I interviewed you after each game to get your opinion on how it all went down?

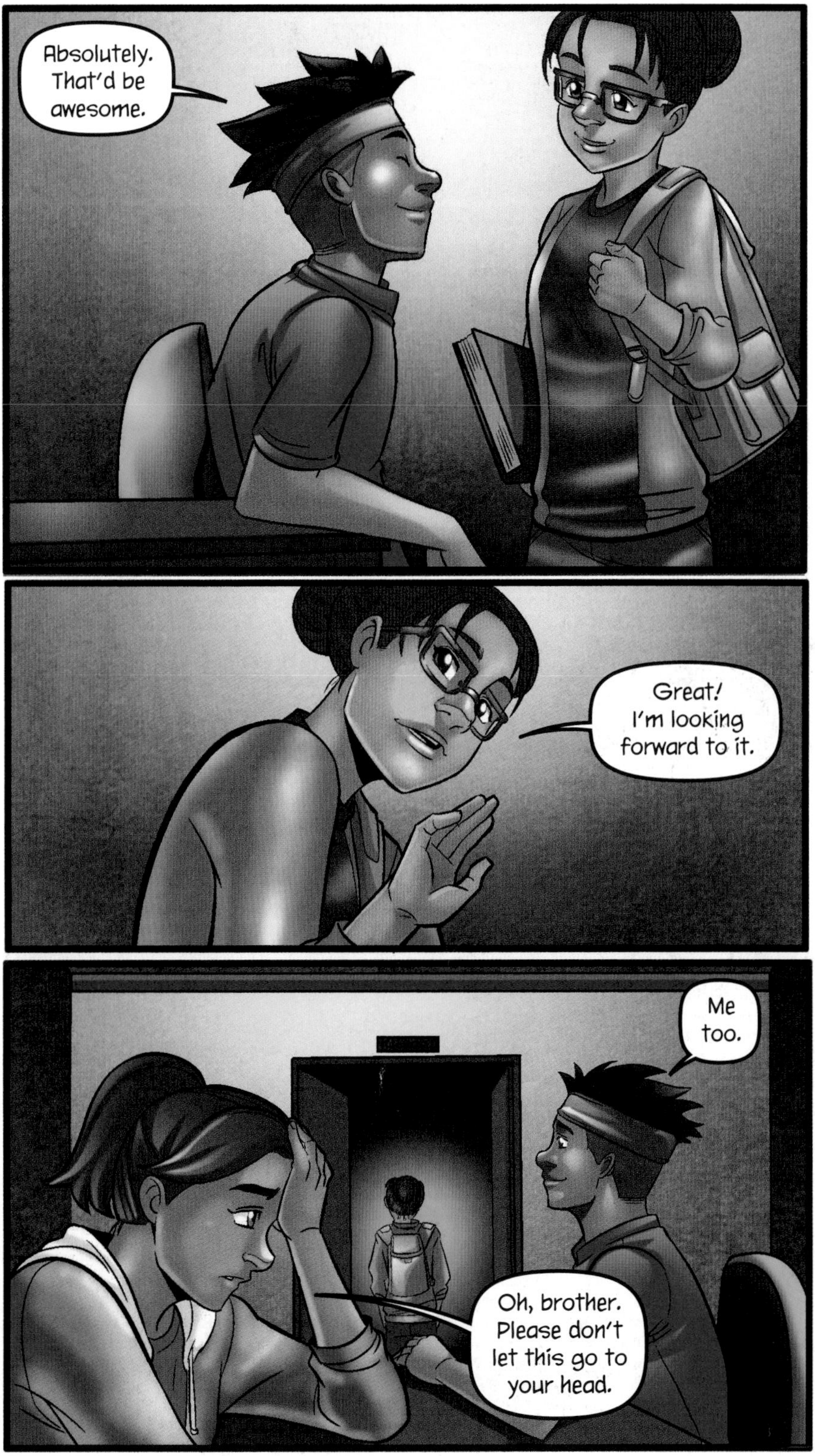
Absolutely. That'd be awesome.
Great! I'm looking forward to it.
Me too.
Oh, brother. Please don't let this go to your head.

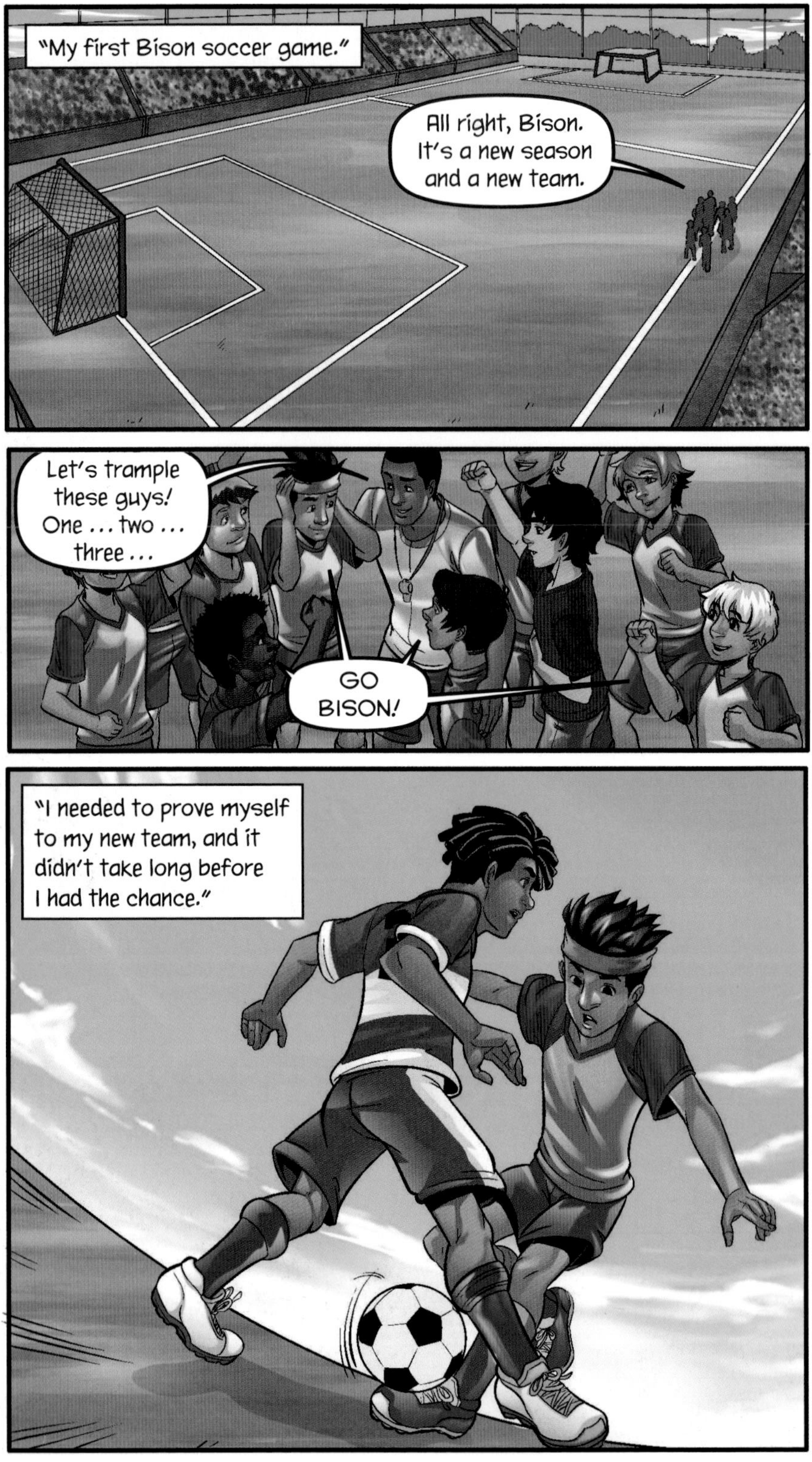
"My first Bison soccer game."
All right, Bison. It's a new season and a new team.
Let's trample these guys! One ... two ... three ...
GO BISON!
"I needed to prove myself to my new team, and it didn't take long before I had the chance."

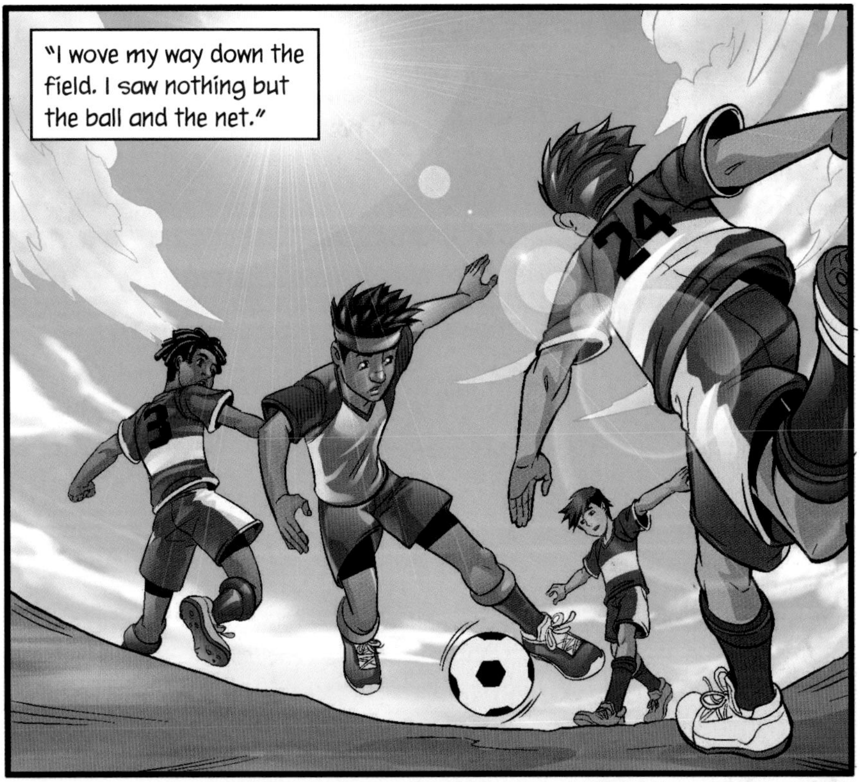
"I wove my way down the field. I saw nothing but the ball and the net."
24
3

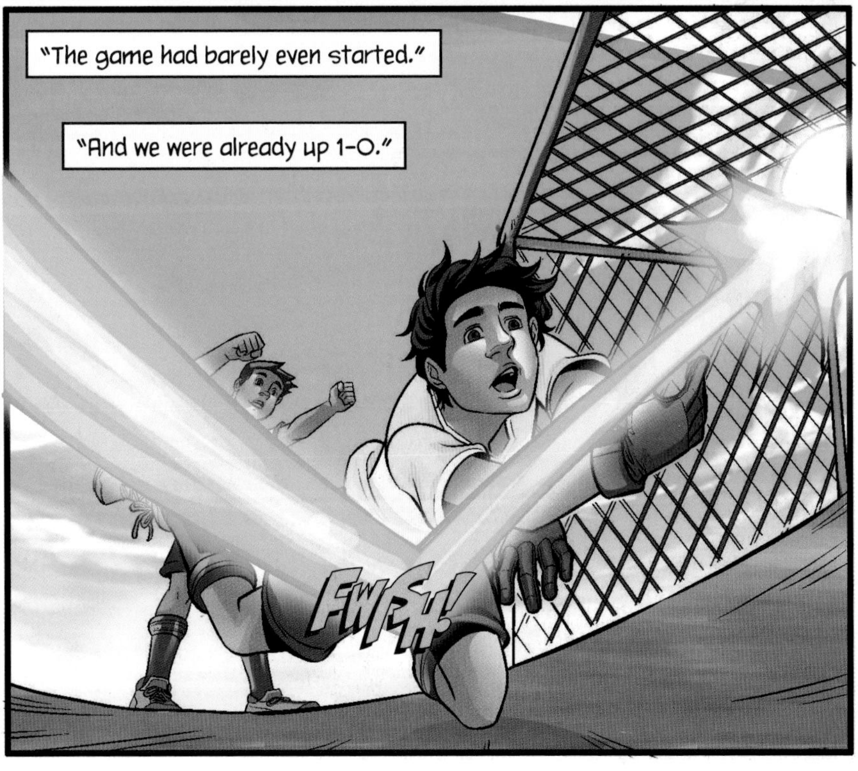
"The game had barely even started."
"And we were already up 1–0."
FWISH!

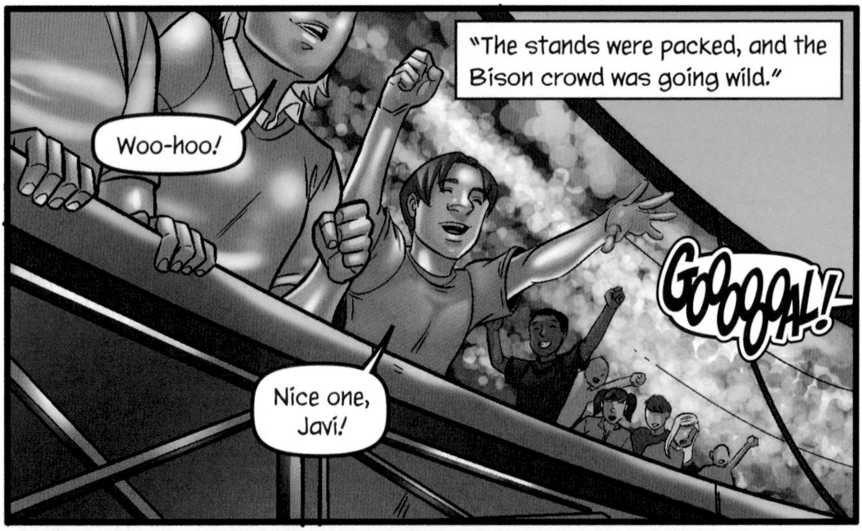
"The stands were packed, and the Bison crowd was going wild."
Woo-hoo!
GOOOOOAL!
Nice one, Javi!

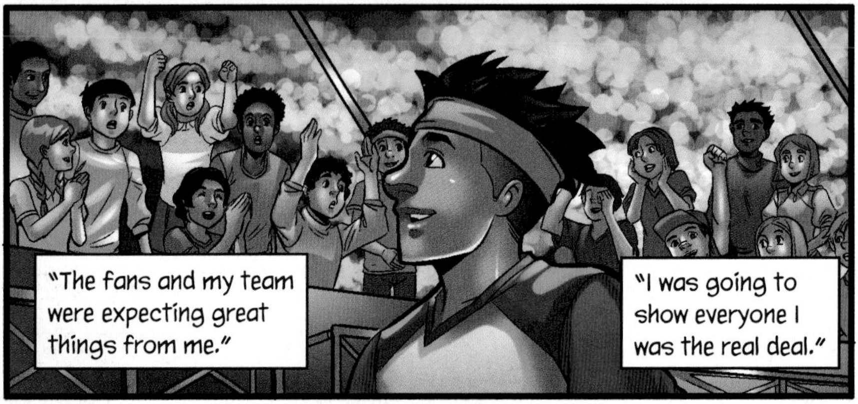
"The fans and my team were expecting great things from me."
"I was going to show everyone I was the real deal."

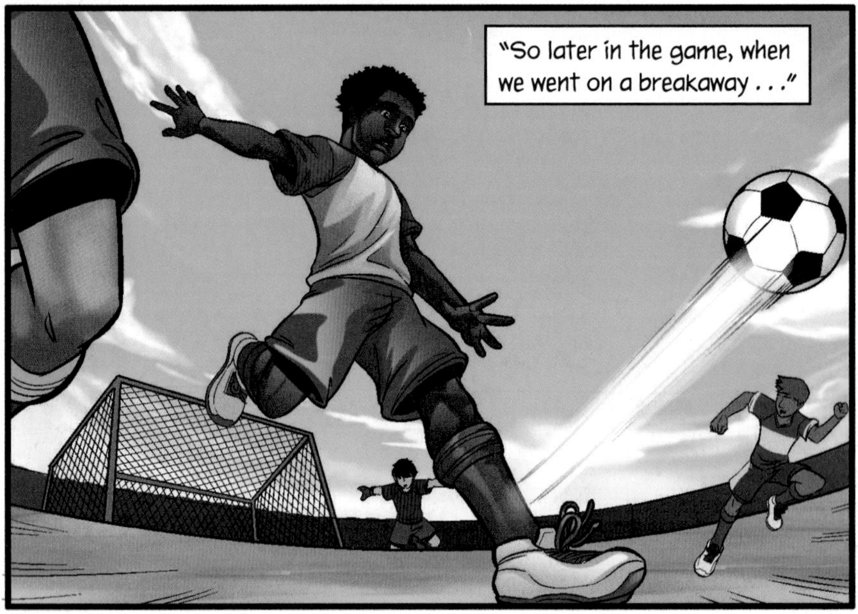
"So later in the game, when we went on a breakaway . . ."

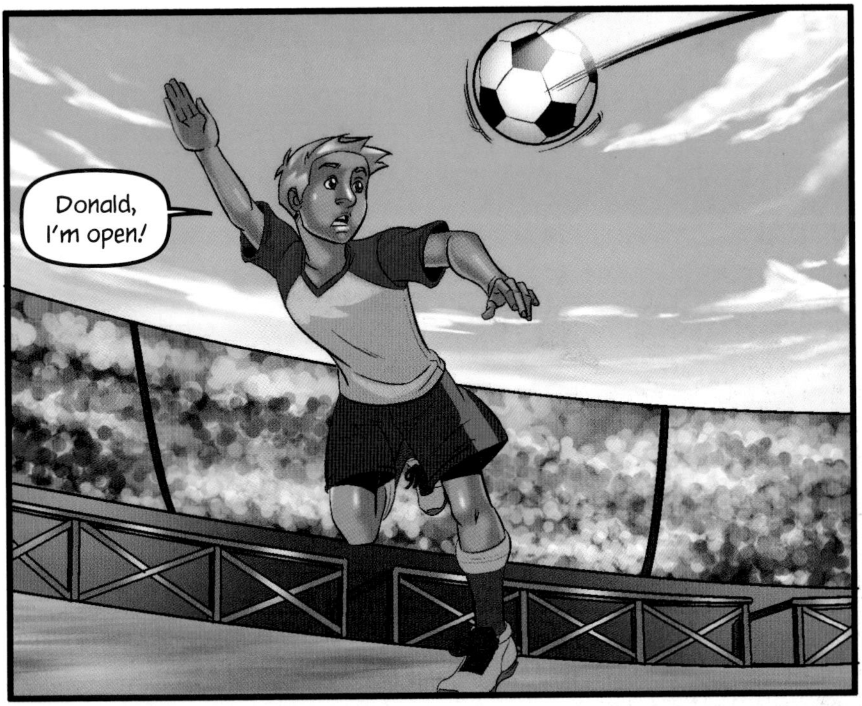
Donald,
I'm open!

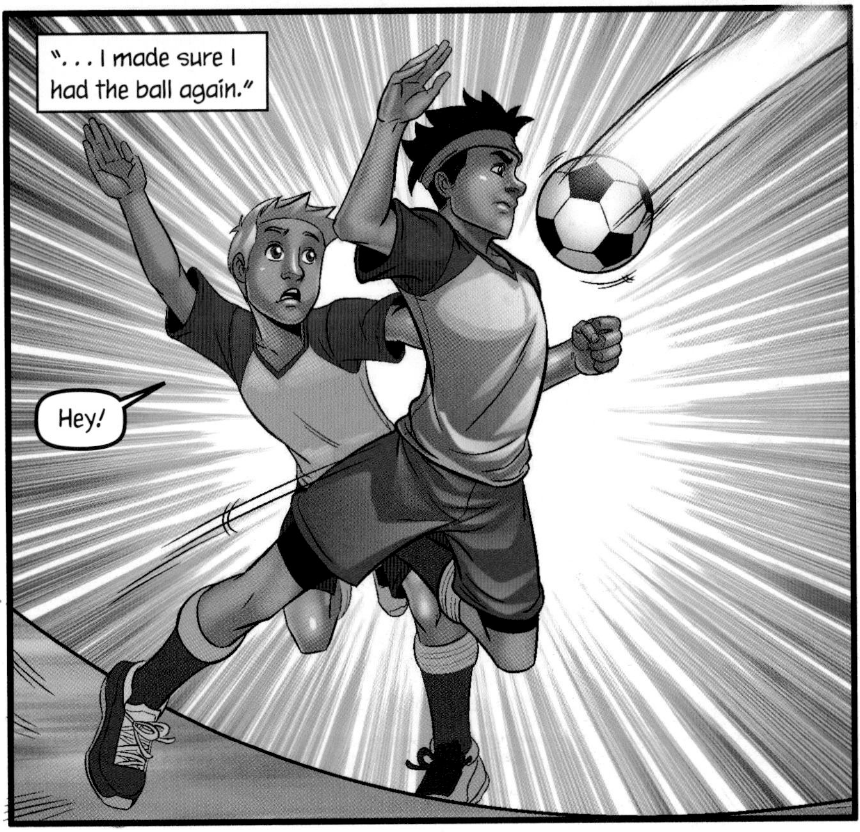
". . . I made sure I
had the ball again."
Hey!

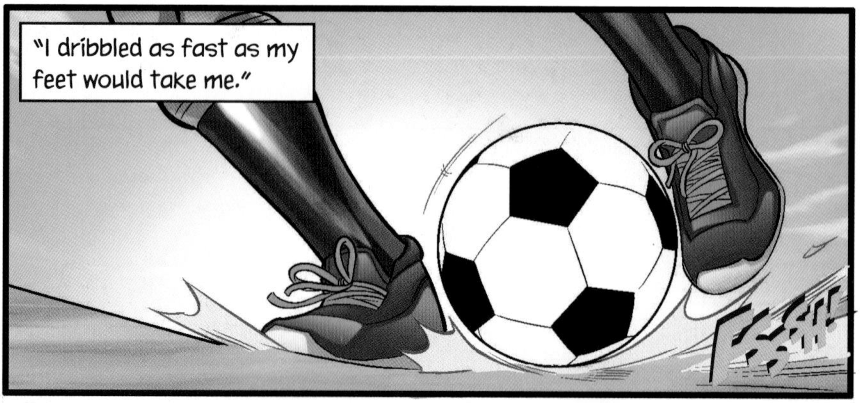
"I dribbled as fast as my feet would take me."
FSSH!

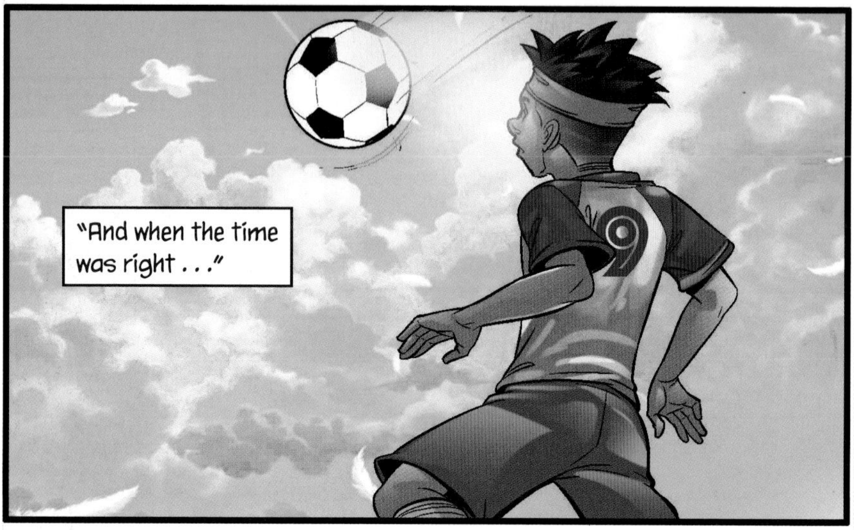
"And when the time was right . . ."

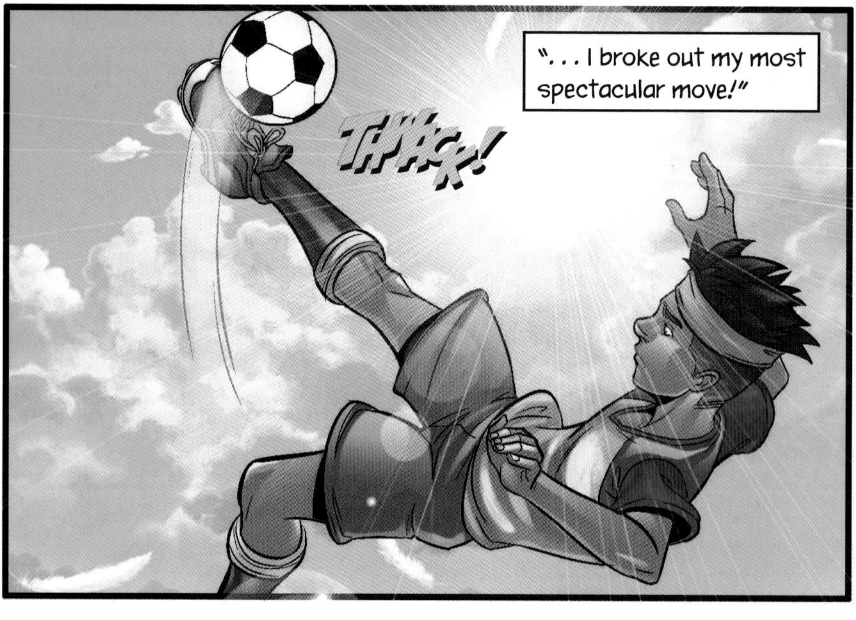
". . . I broke out my most spectacular move!"
THWACK!

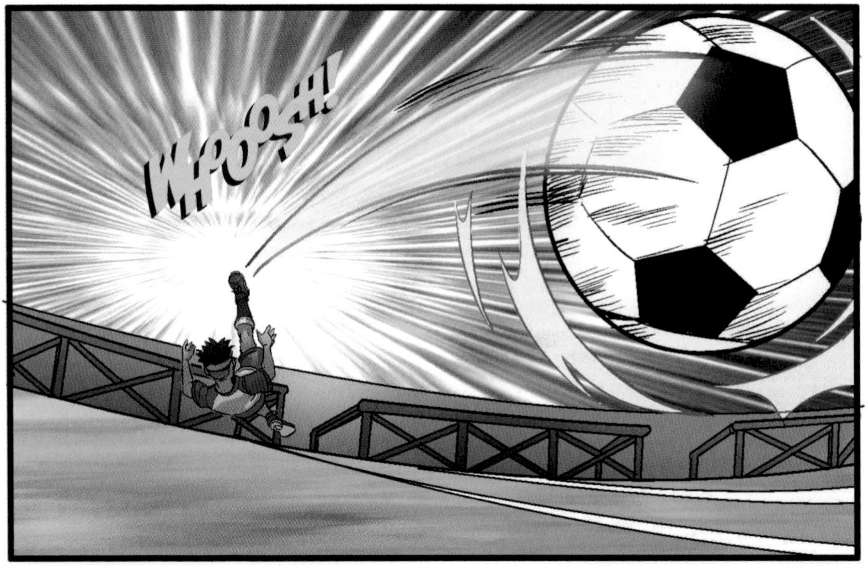
WHOOSH!

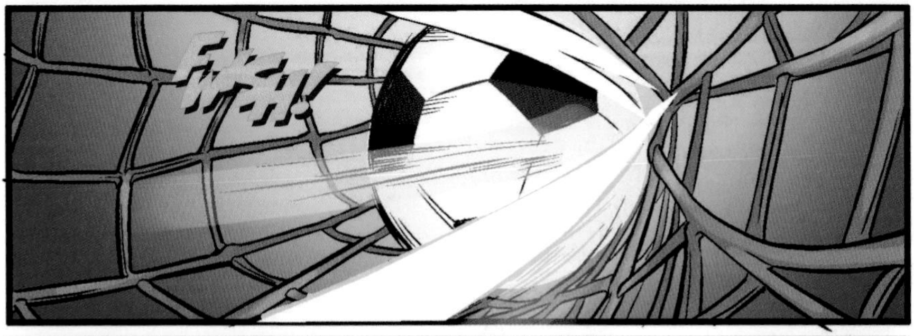

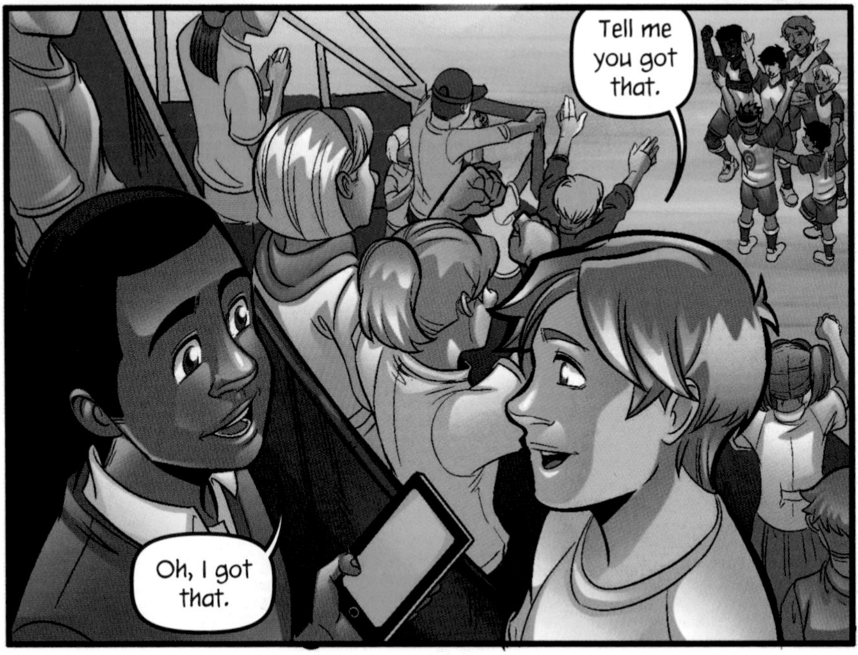
Tell me you got that.
Oh, I got that.

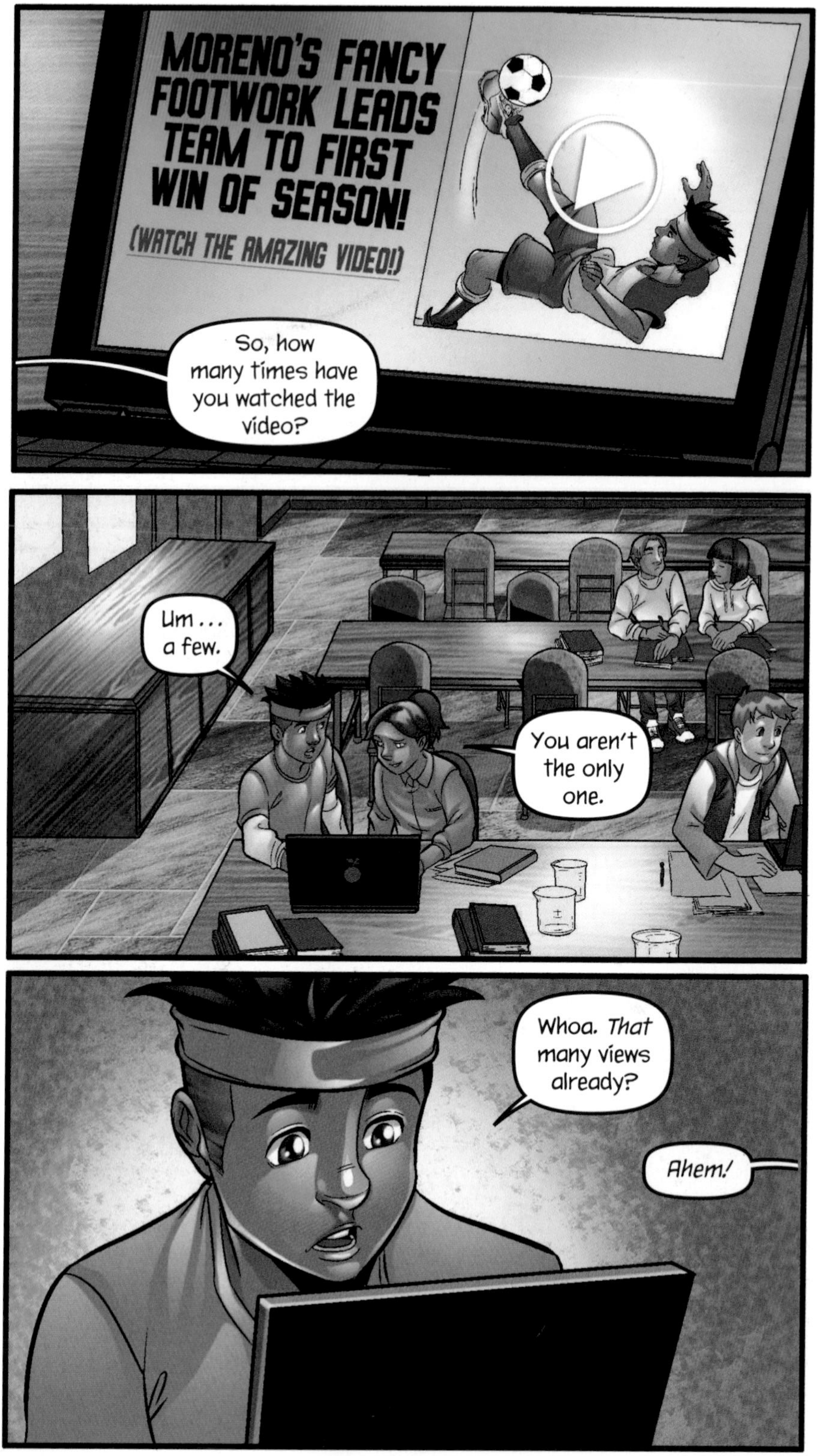
MORENO'S FANCY FOOTWORK LEADS TEAM TO FIRST WIN OF SEASON!
(WATCH THE AMAZING VIDEO!)
So, how many times have you watched the video?
Um . . . a few.
You aren't the only one.
Whoa. *That* many views already?
Ahem!

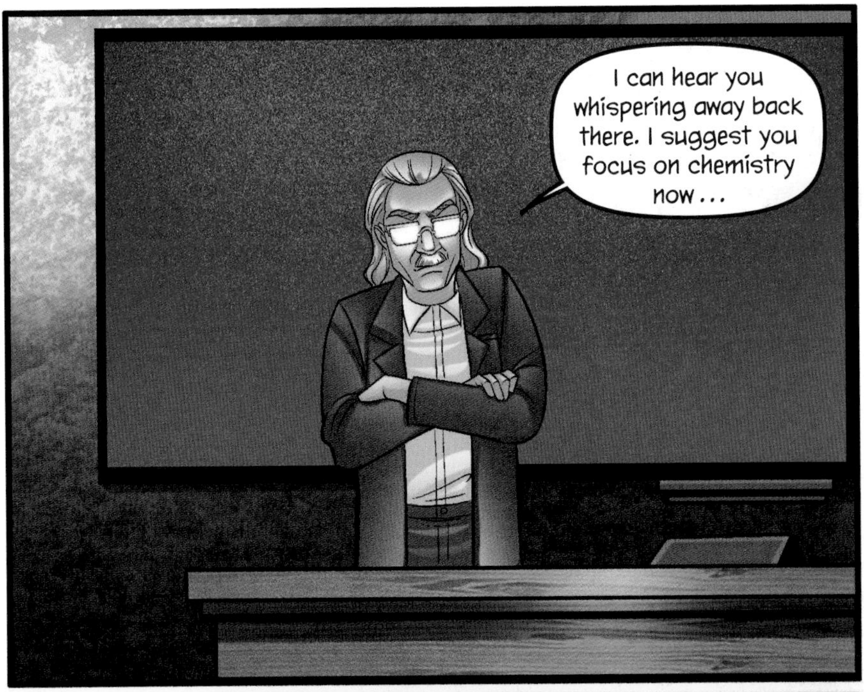
I can hear you whispering away back there. I suggest you focus on chemistry now . . .

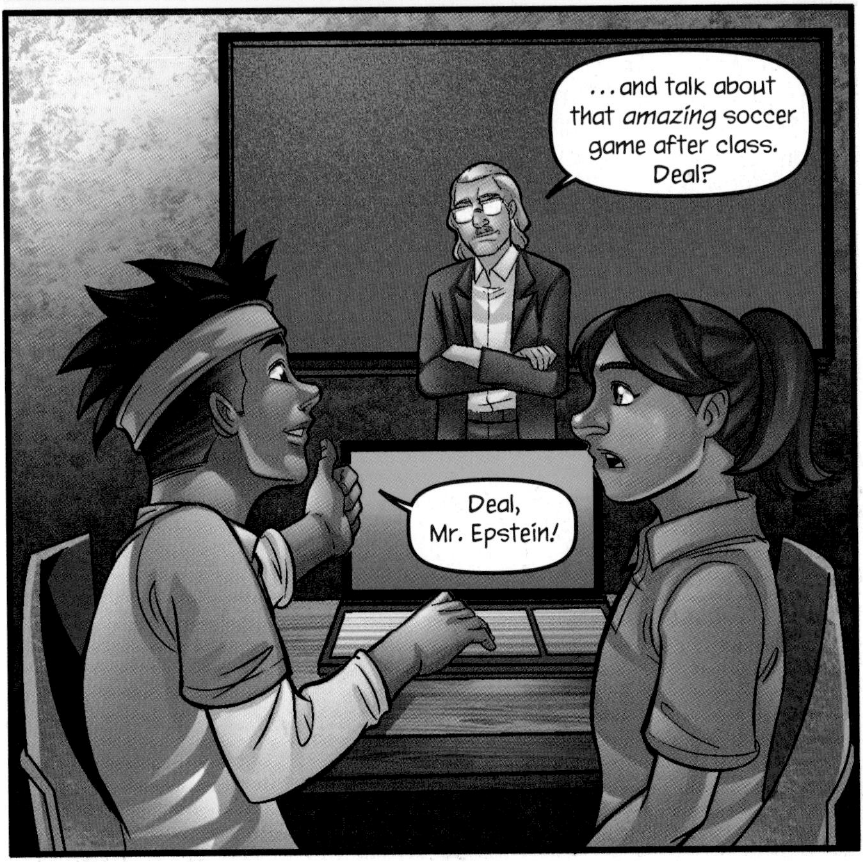
. . . and talk about that *amazing* soccer game after class. Deal?
Deal, Mr. Epstein!

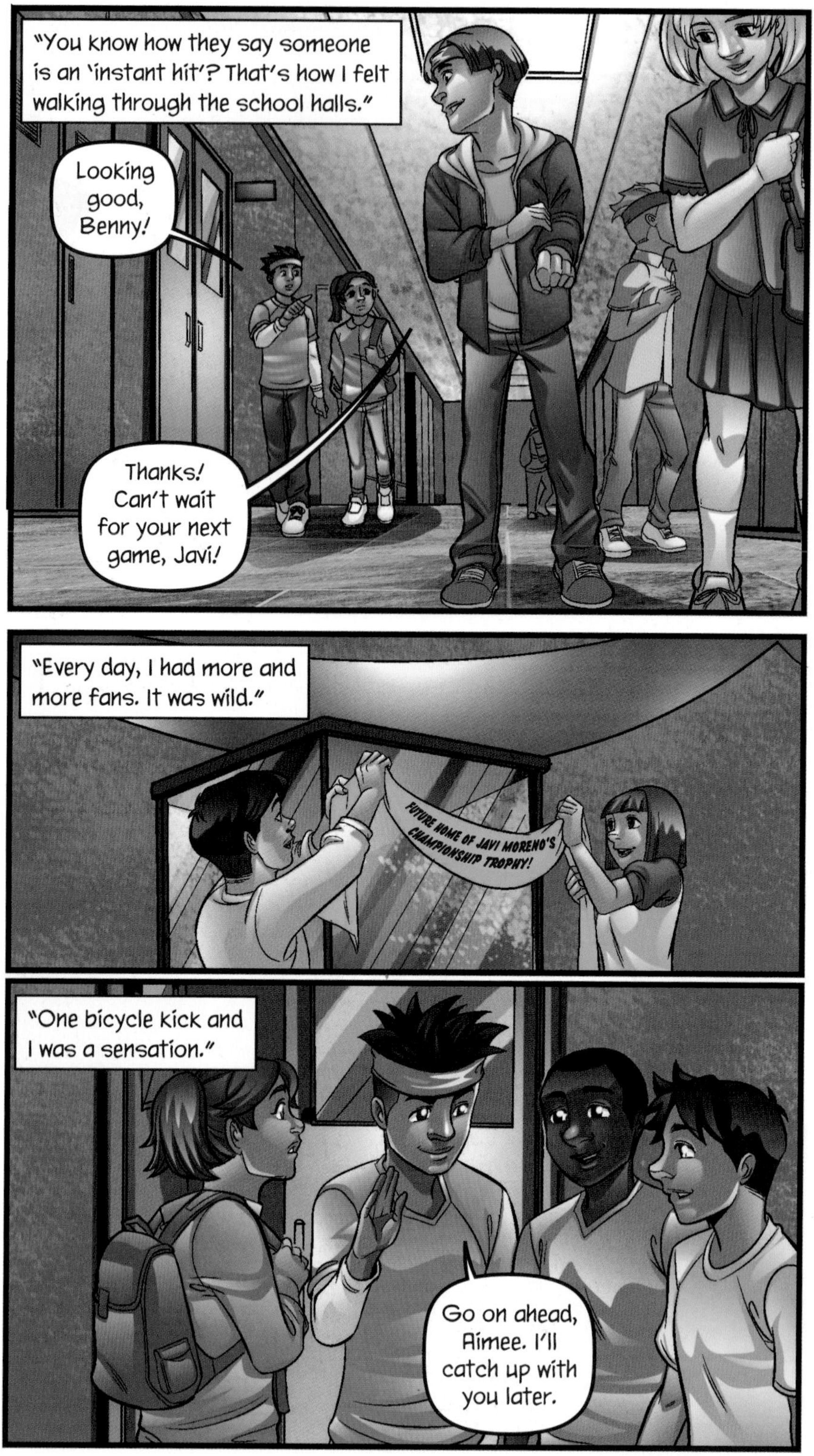
"You know how they say someone is an 'instant hit'? That's how I felt walking through the school halls."
Looking good, Benny!
Thanks! Can't wait for your next game, Javi!
"Every day, I had more and more fans. It was wild."
FUTURE HOME OF JAVI MORENO'S CHAMPIONSHIP TROPHY!
"One bicycle kick and I was a sensation."
Go on ahead, Aimee. I'll catch up with you later.

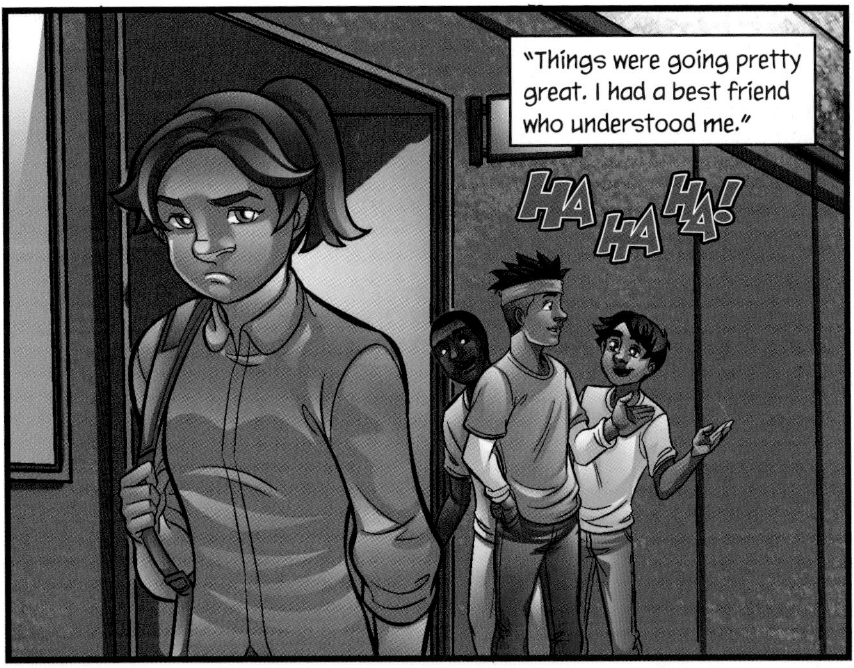
"Things were going pretty great. I had a best friend who understood me."
HA HA HA!

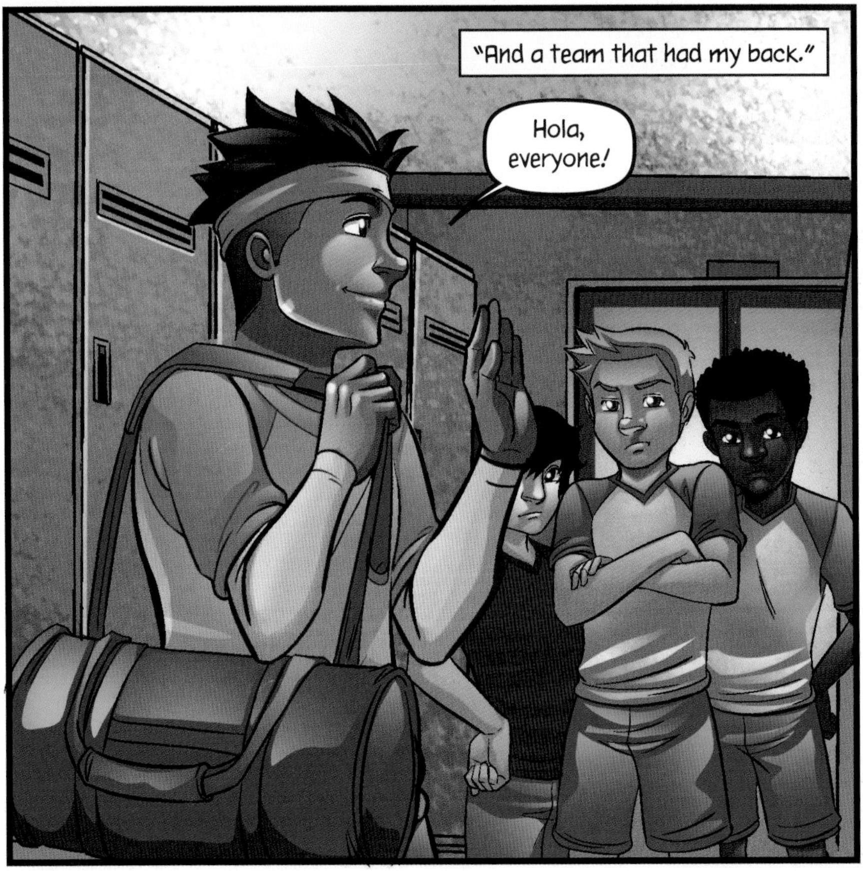
"And a team that had my back."
Hola, everyone!

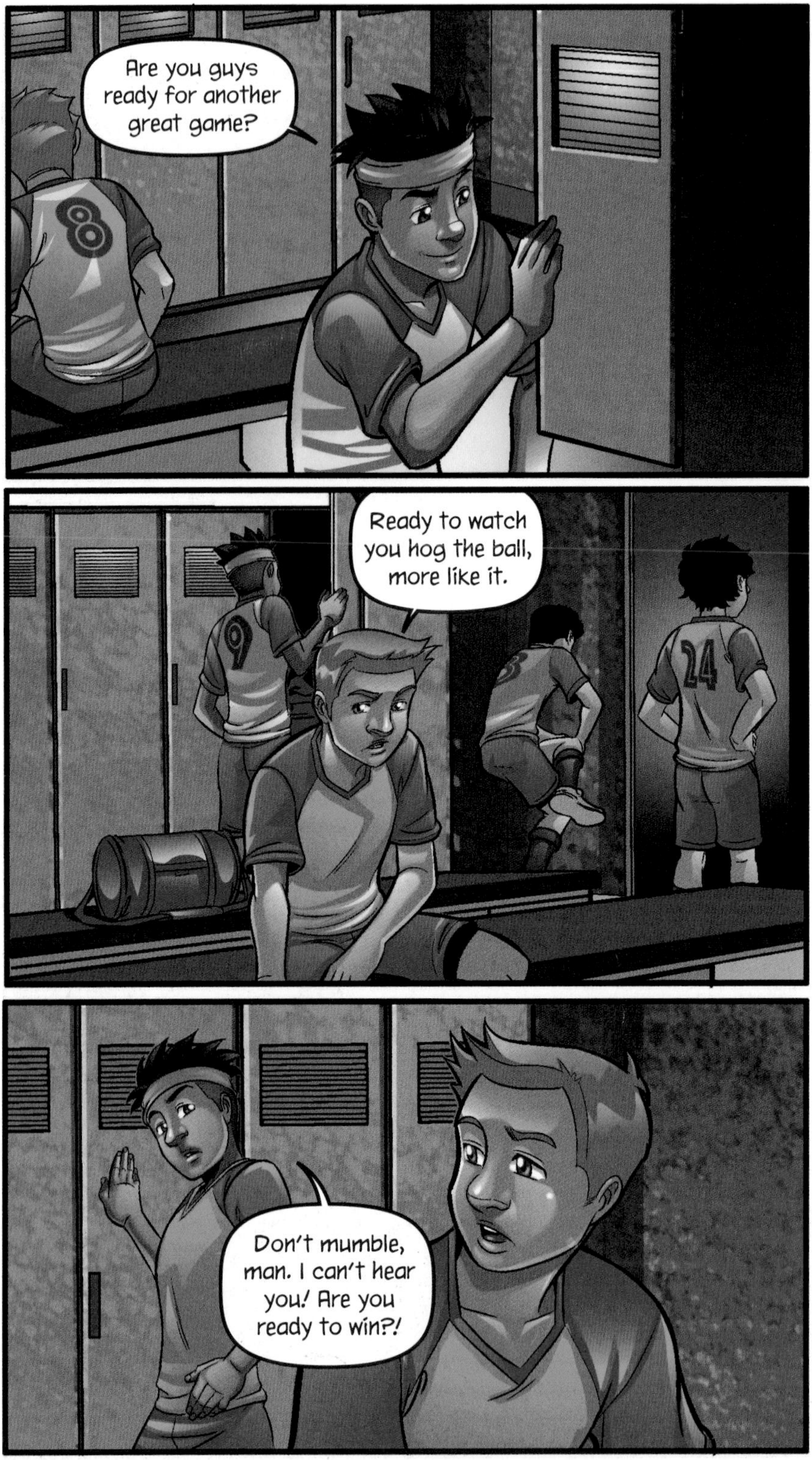
Are you guys ready for another great game?
Ready to watch you hog the ball, more like it.
Don't mumble, man. I can't hear you! Are you ready to win?!

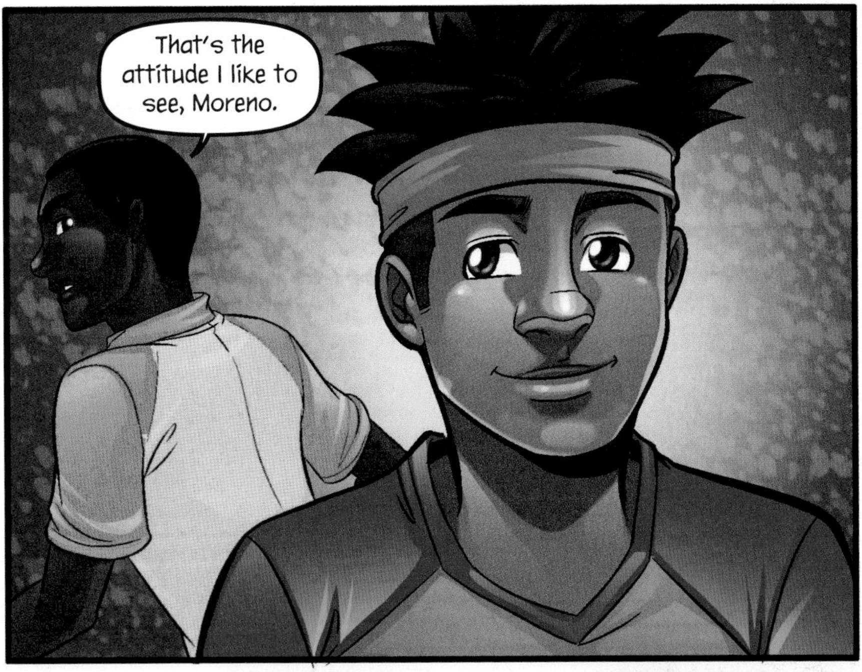
That's the attitude I like to see, Moreno.

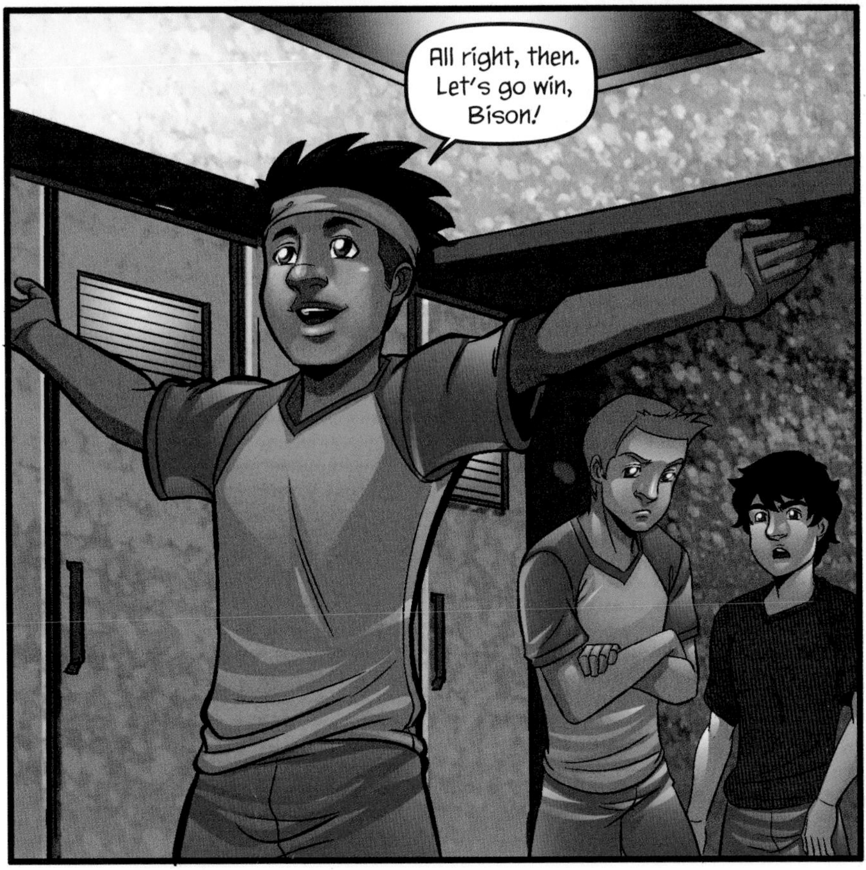
All right, then. Let's go win, Bison!

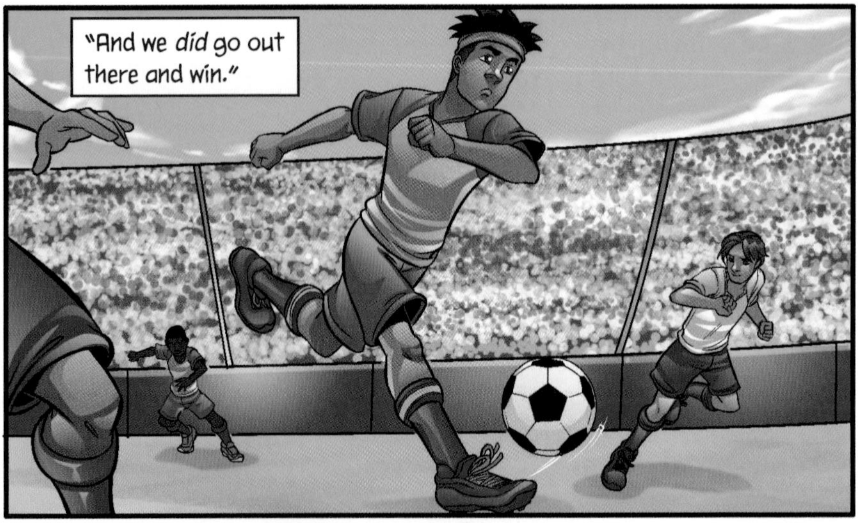
"And we *did* go out there and win."

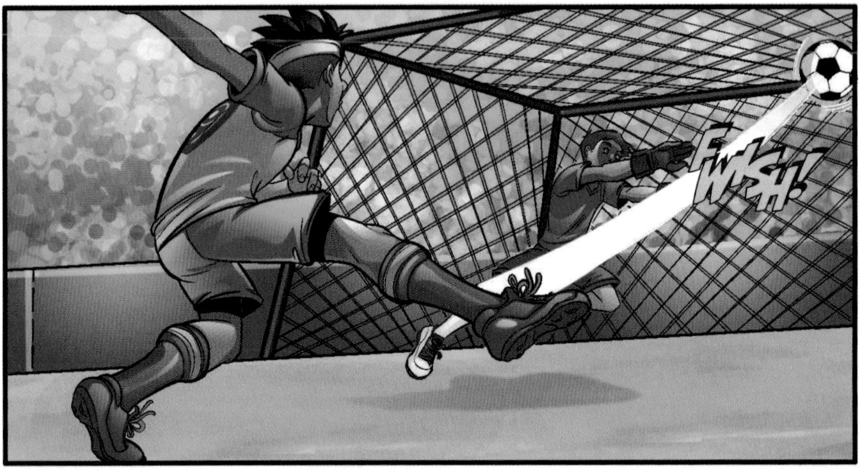
FWISH!

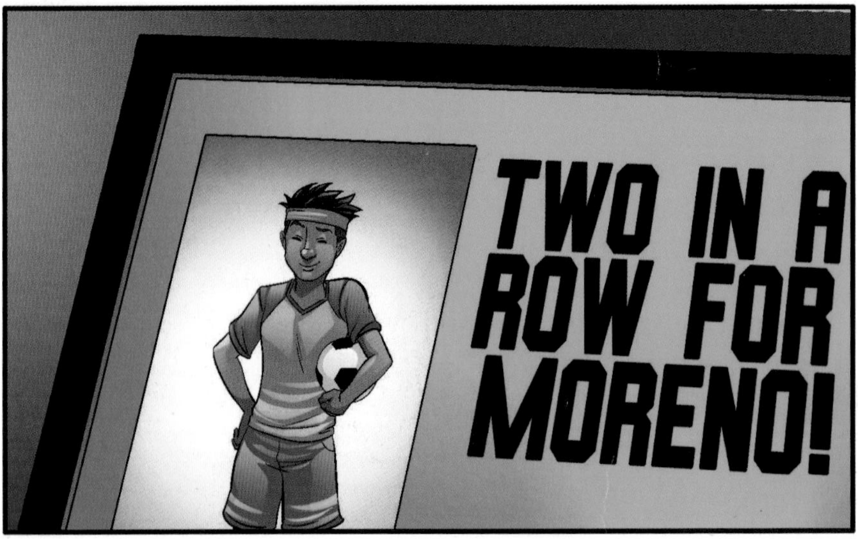
TWO IN A ROW FOR MORENO!

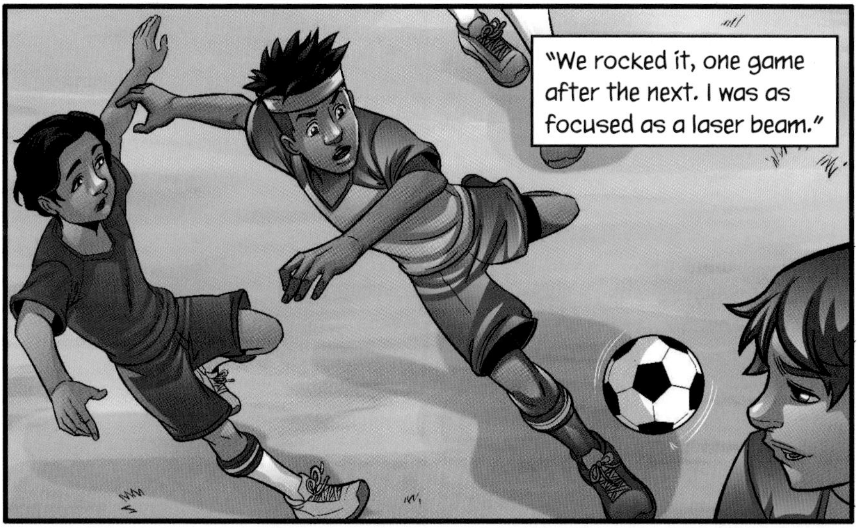
"We rocked it, one game after the next. I was as focused as a laser beam."

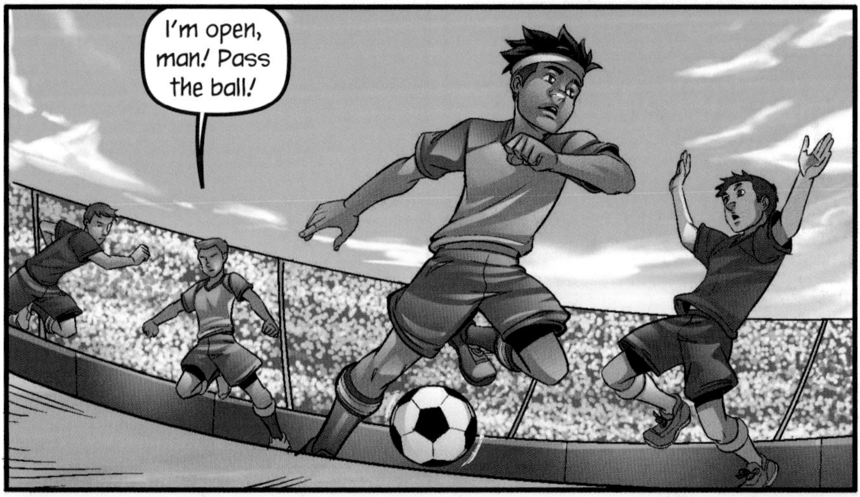
I'm open, man! Pass the ball!

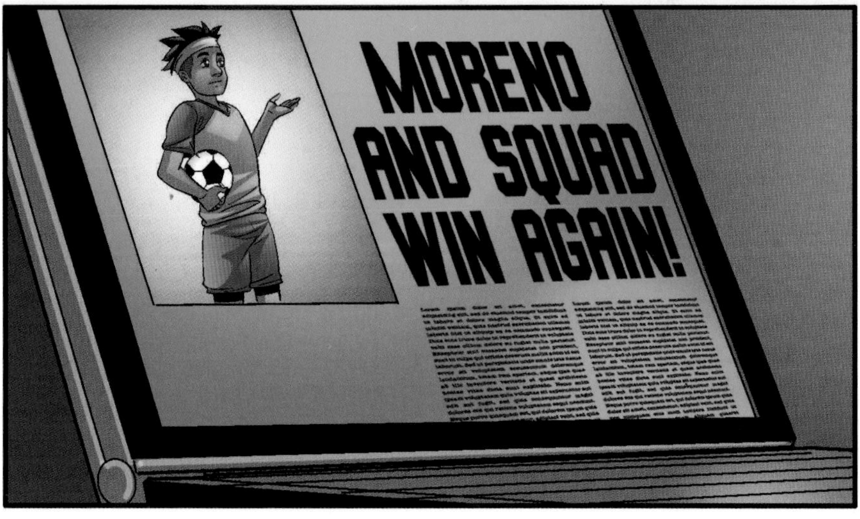
MORENO AND SQUAD WIN AGAIN!

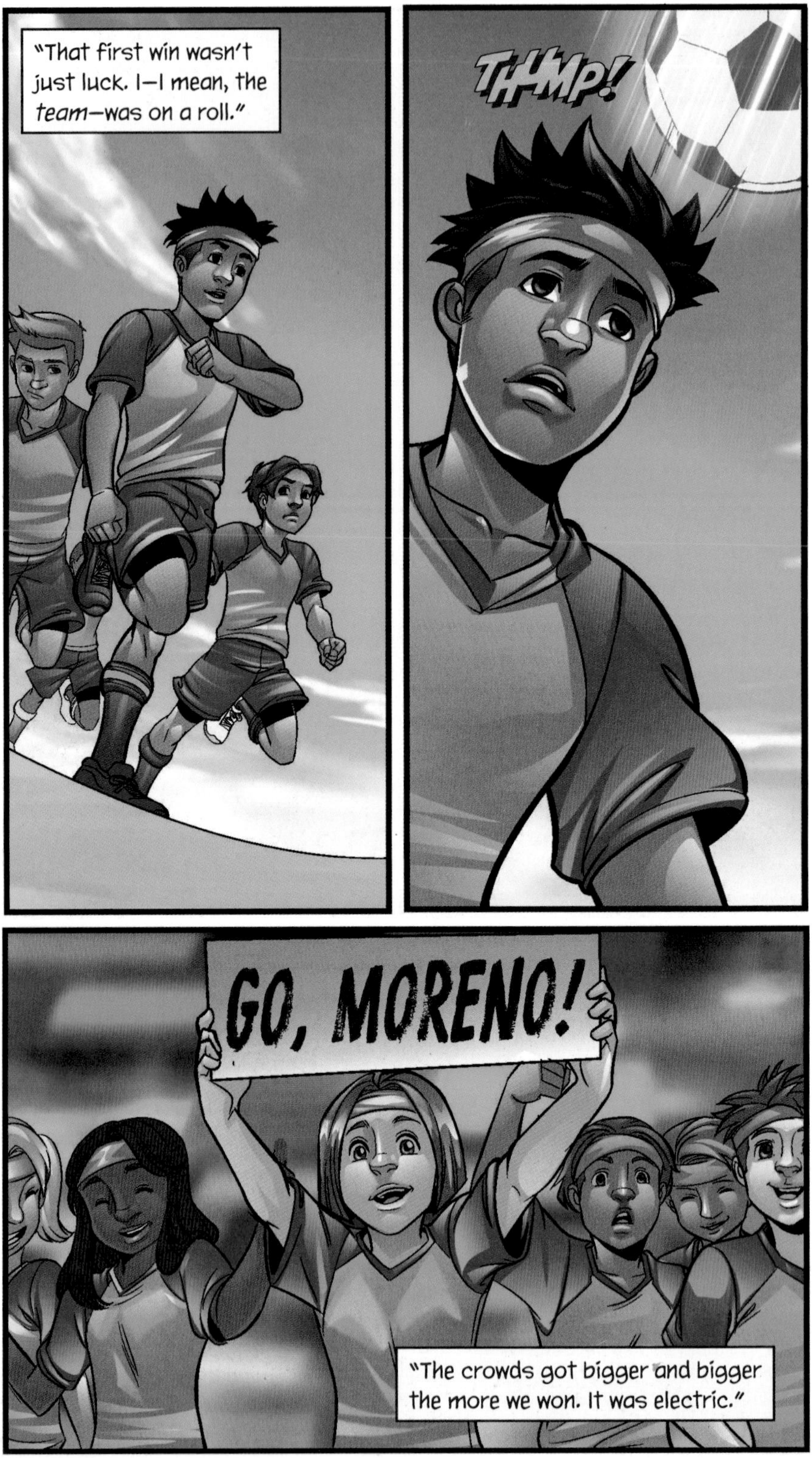
"That first win wasn't just luck. I—I mean, the *team*—was on a roll."
THUMP!
GO, MORENO!
"The crowds got bigger and bigger the more we won. It was electric."

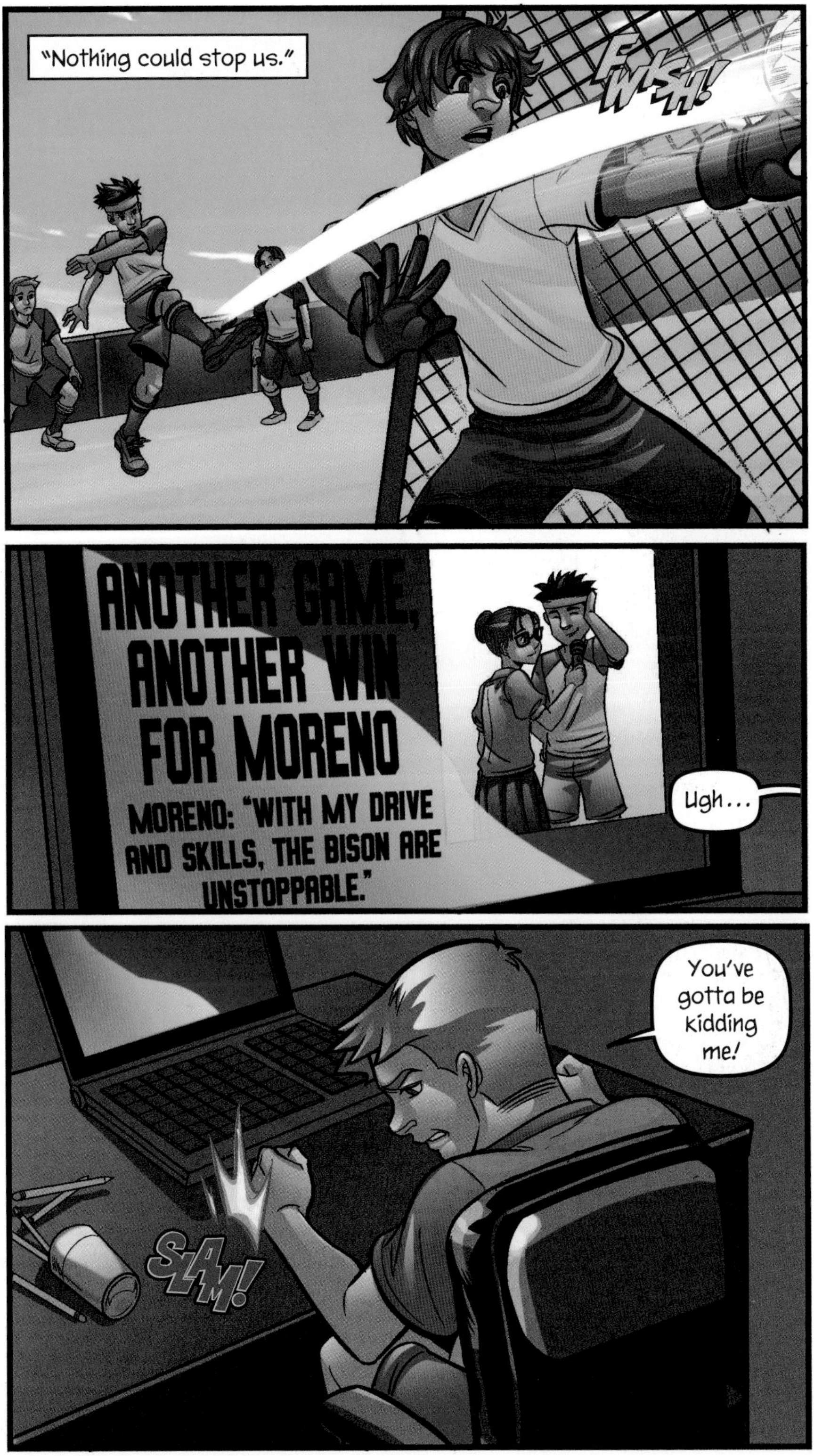
"Nothing could stop us."
FWISH!
ANOTHER GAME, ANOTHER WIN FOR MORENO
MORENO: "WITH MY DRIVE AND SKILLS, THE BISON ARE UNSTOPPABLE."
Ugh...
You've gotta be kidding me!
SLAM!

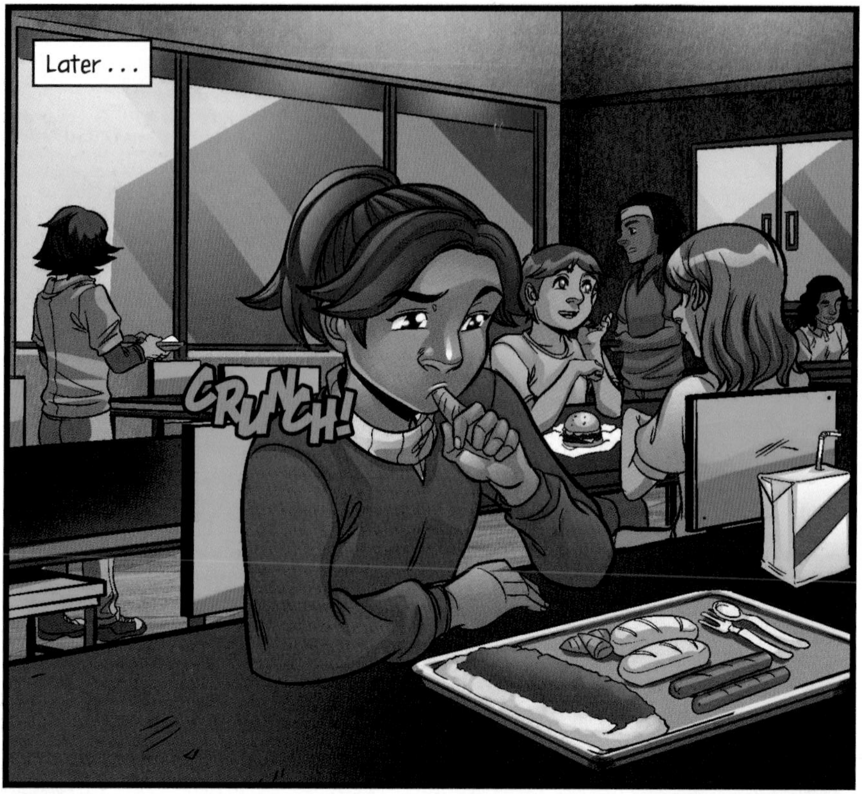
Later . . .
CRUNCH!

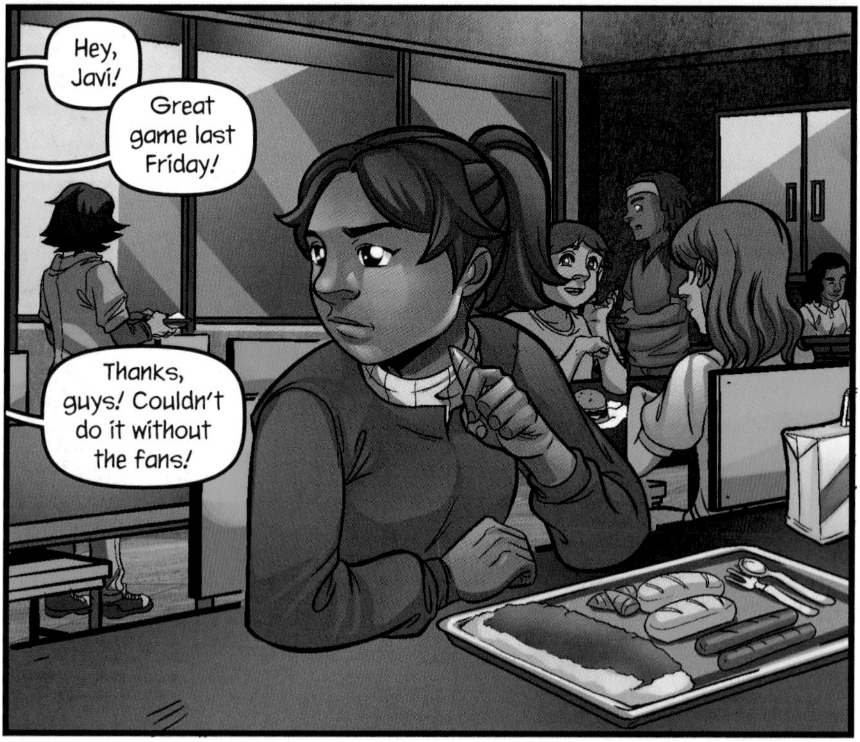
Hey, Javi!
Great game last Friday!
Thanks, guys! Couldn't do it without the fans!

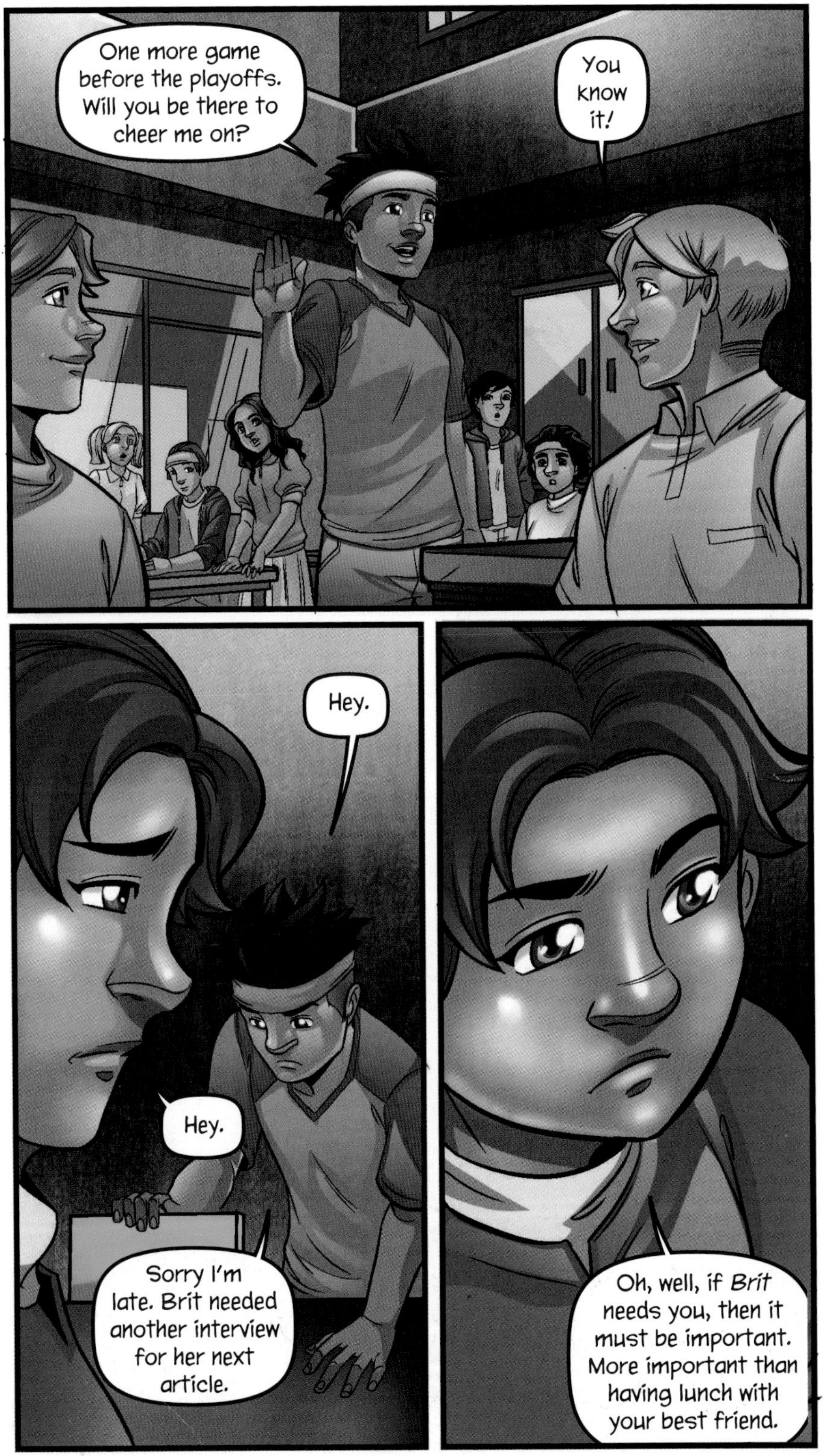
One more game before the playoffs. Will you be there to cheer me on?
You know it!
Hey.
Hey.
Sorry I'm late. Brit needed another interview for her next article.
Oh, well, if *Brit* needs you, then it must be important. More important than having lunch with your best friend.

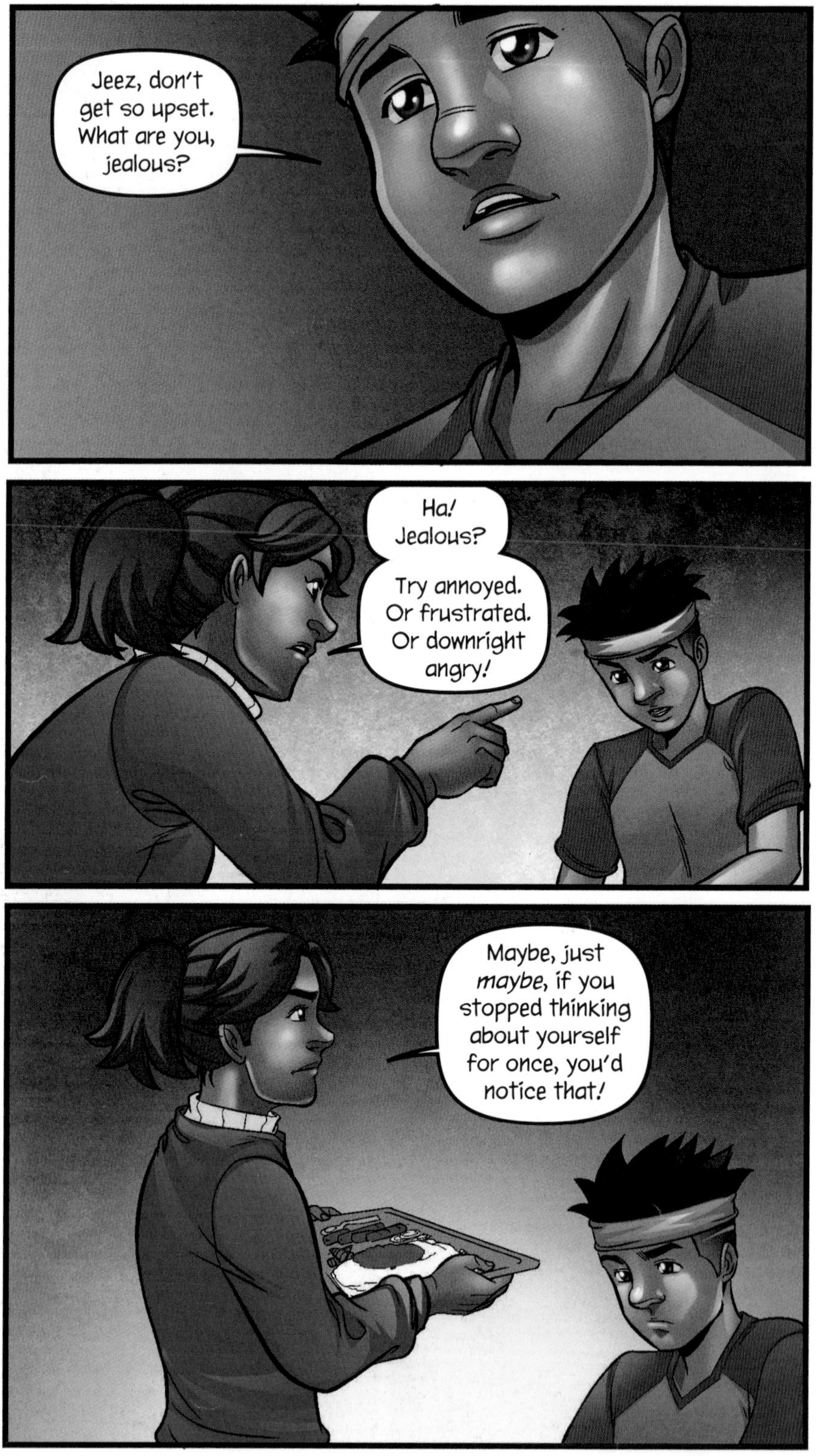
Jeez, don't get so upset. What are you, jealous?
Ha! Jealous?
Try annoyed. Or frustrated. Or downright angry!
Maybe, just *maybe*, if you stopped thinking about yourself for once, you'd notice that!

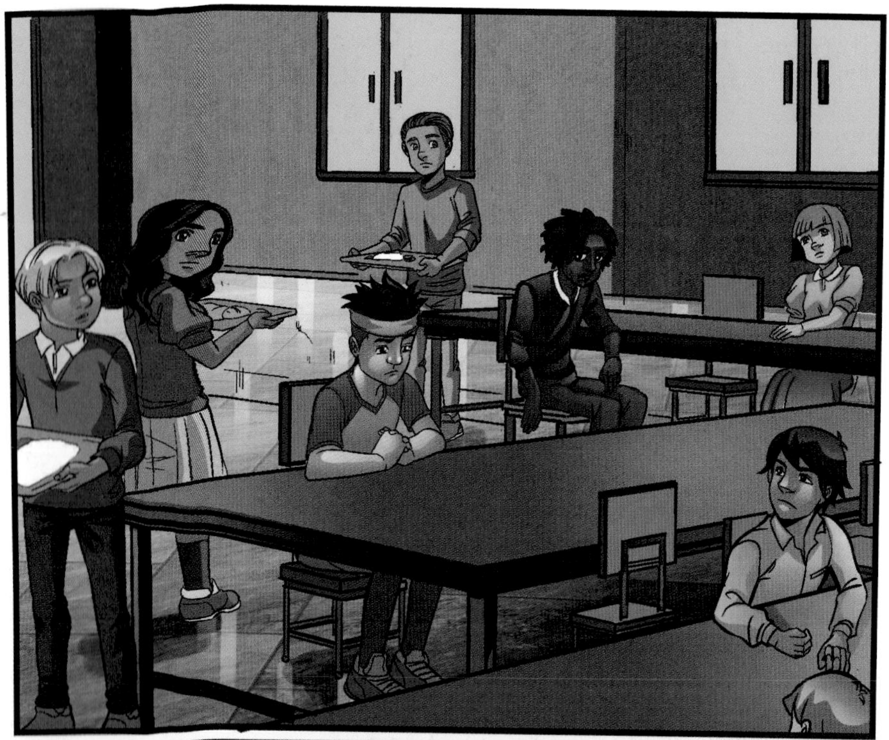

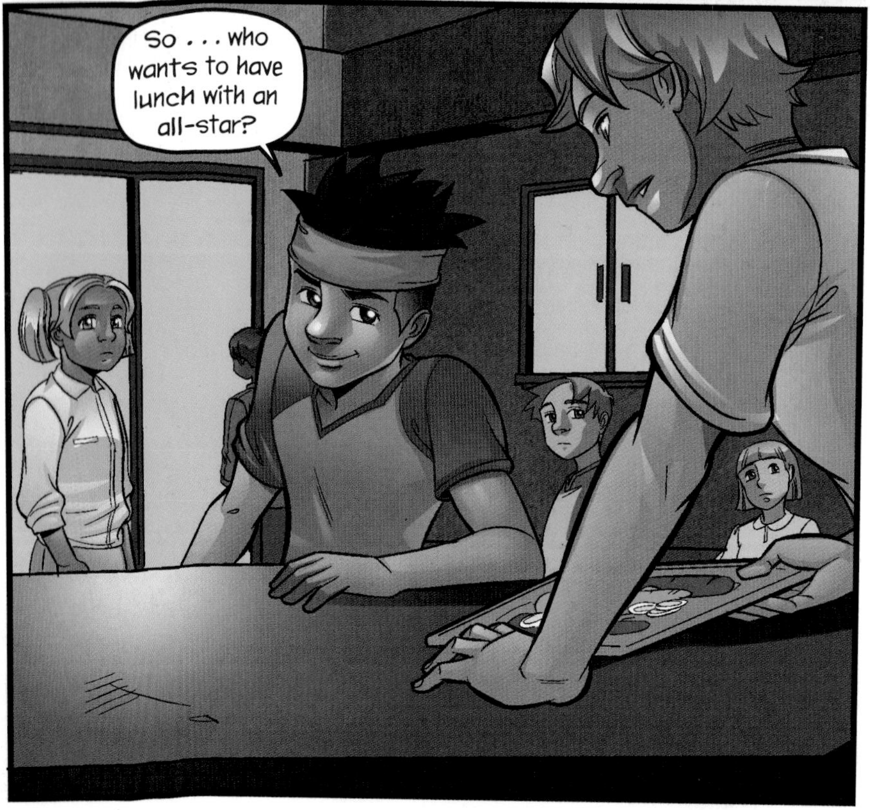
So . . . who wants to have lunch with an all-star?

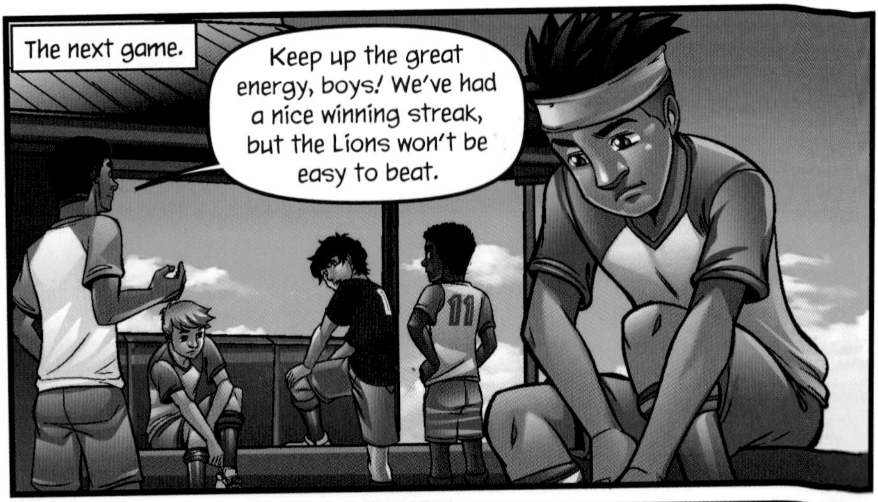
The next game.
Keep up the great energy, boys! We've had a nice winning streak, but the Lions won't be easy to beat.

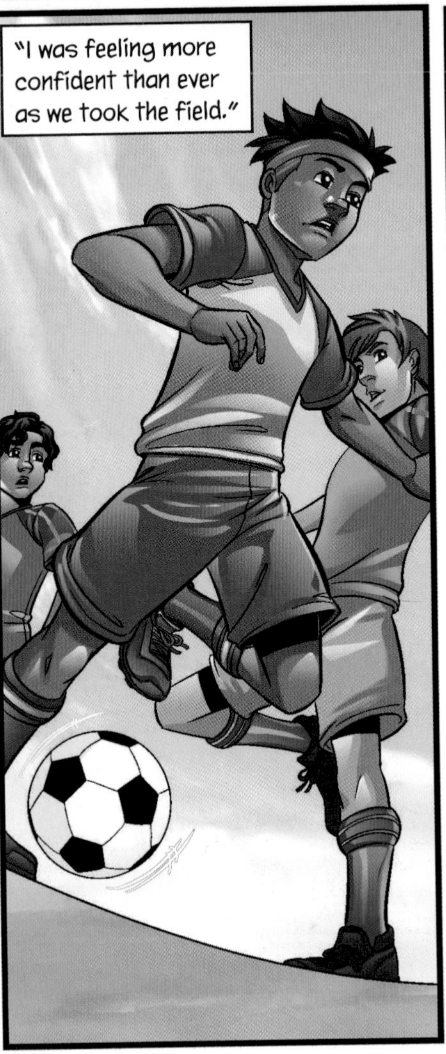
"I was feeling more confident than ever as we took the field."

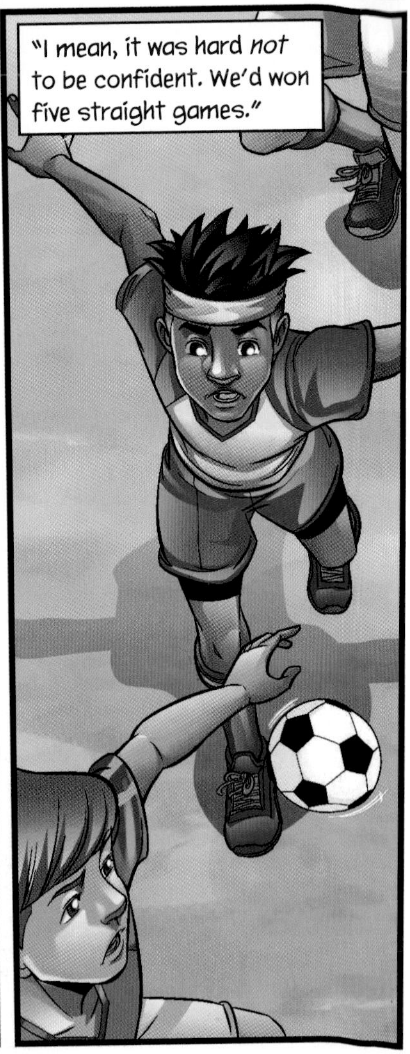
"I mean, it was hard *not* to be confident. We'd won five straight games."

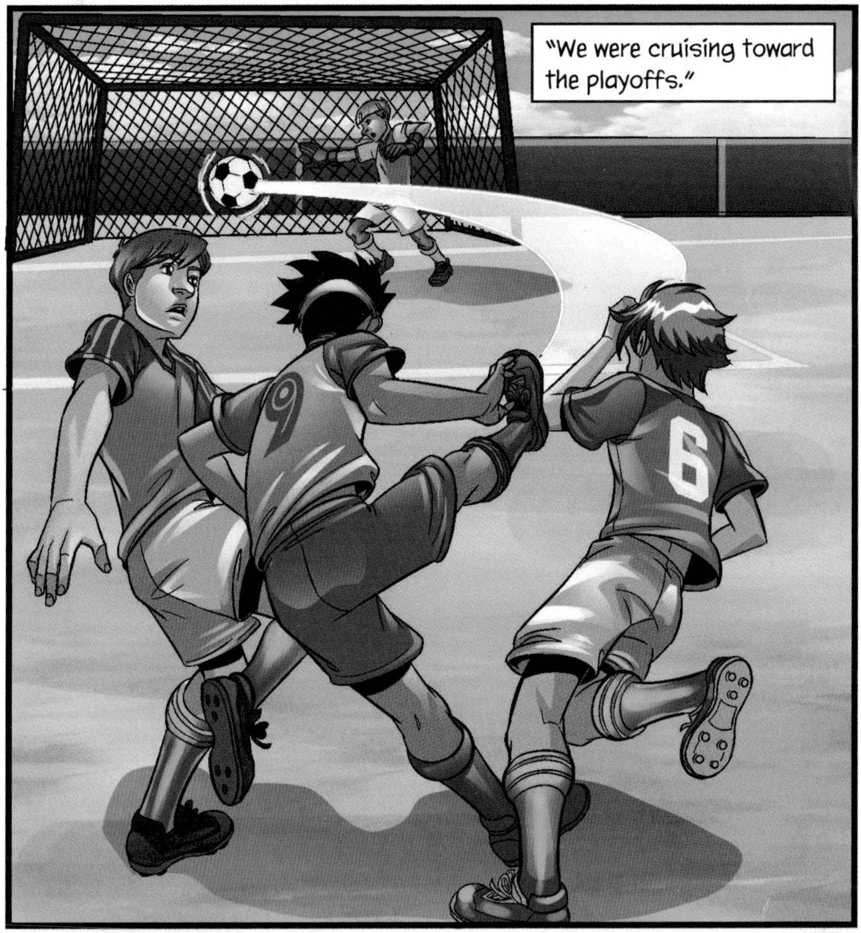
"We were cruising toward the playoffs."

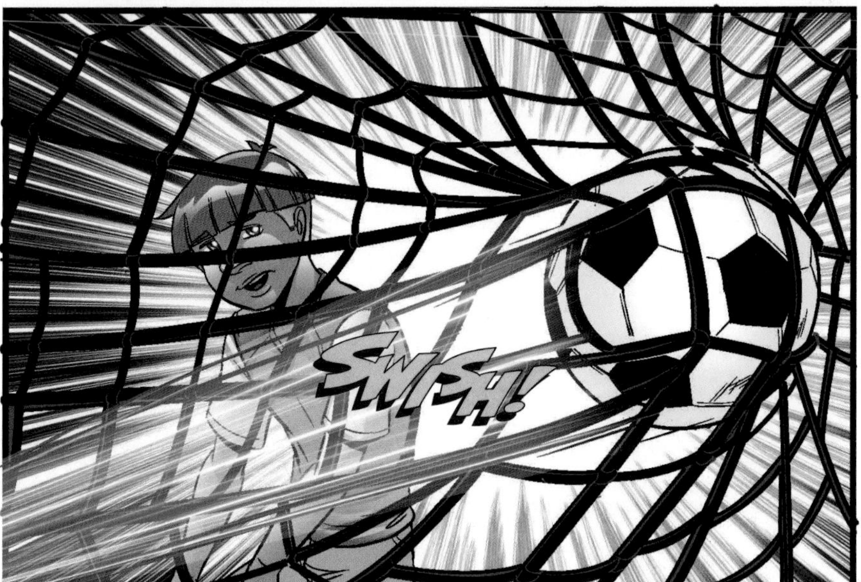
SWISH!

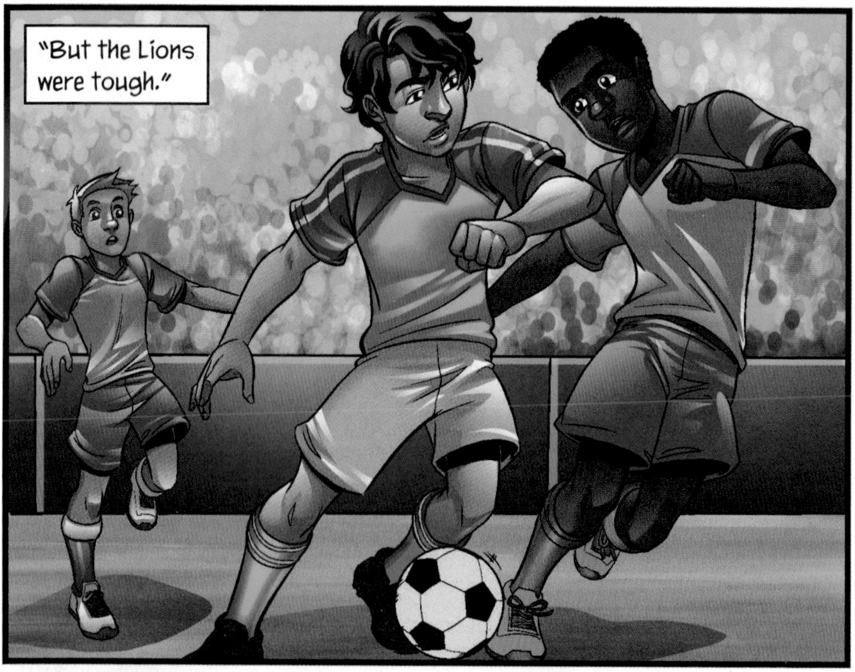
"But the Lions were tough."

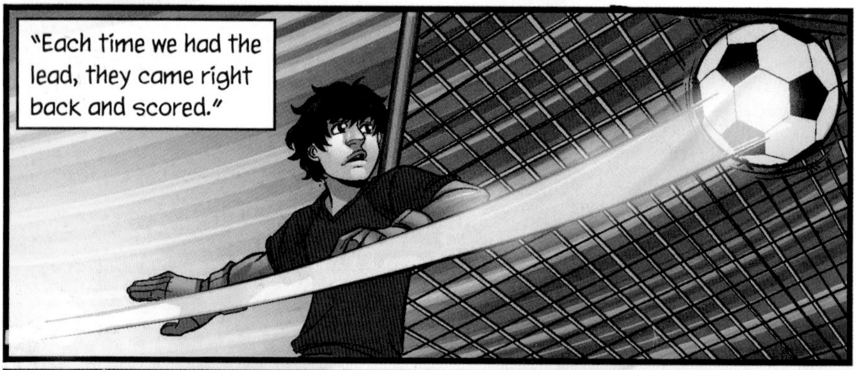
"Each time we had the lead, they came right back and scored."

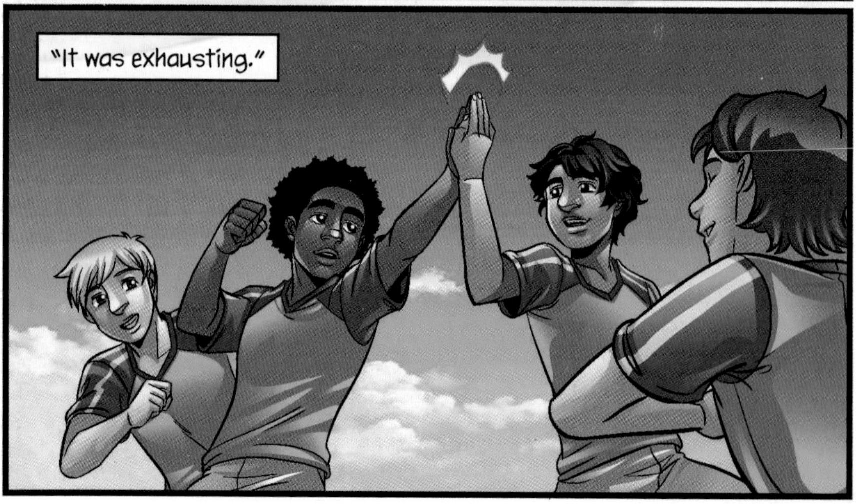
"It was exhausting."

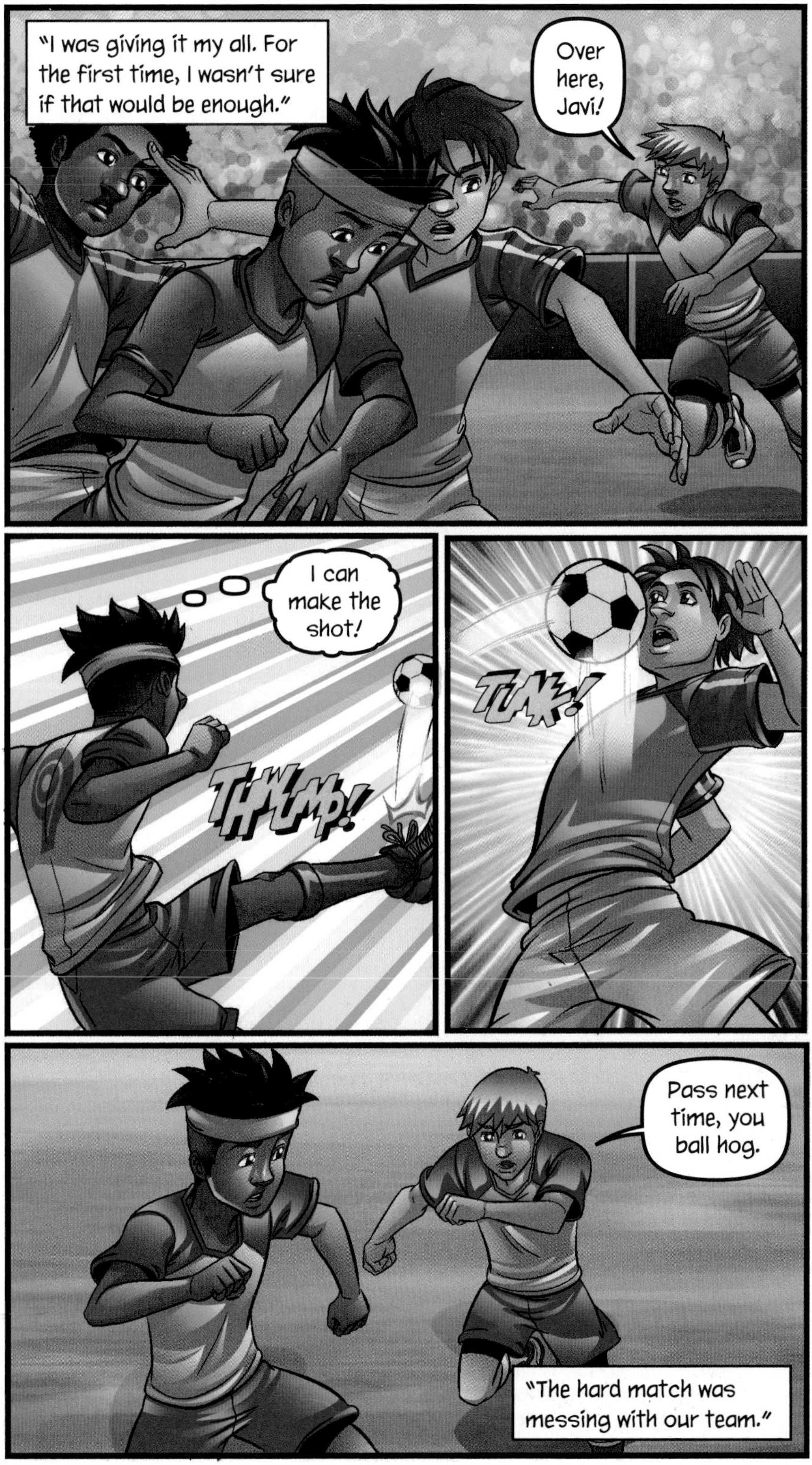
"I was giving it my all. For the first time, I wasn't sure if that would be enough."
Over here, Javi!
I can make the shot!
THWUMP!
TUNK!
Pass next time, you ball hog.
"The hard match was messing with our team."

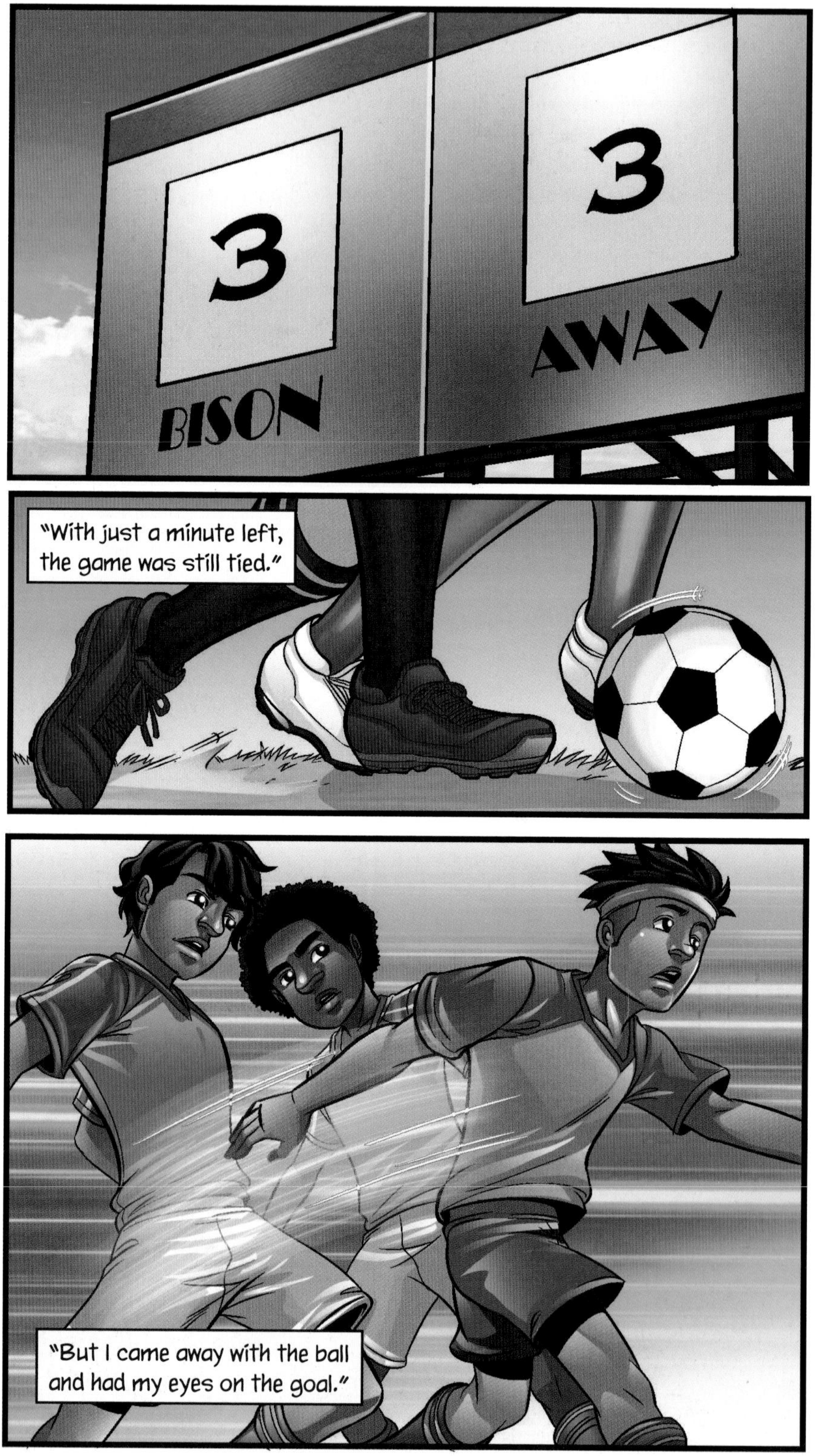
3
BISON
3
AWAY
"With just a minute left, the game was still tied."
"But I came away with the ball and had my eyes on the goal."

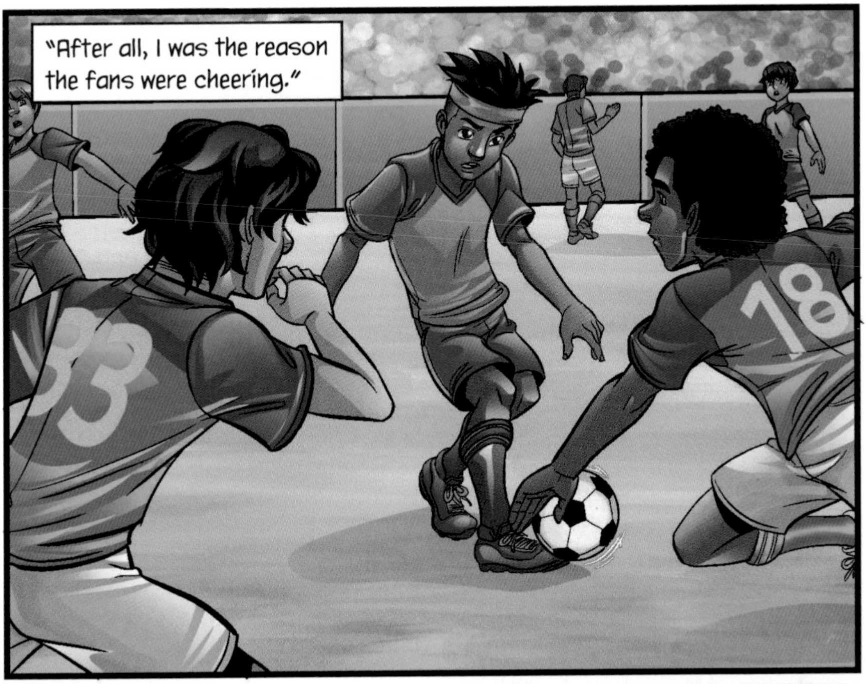
"After all, I was the reason the fans were cheering."
18
33

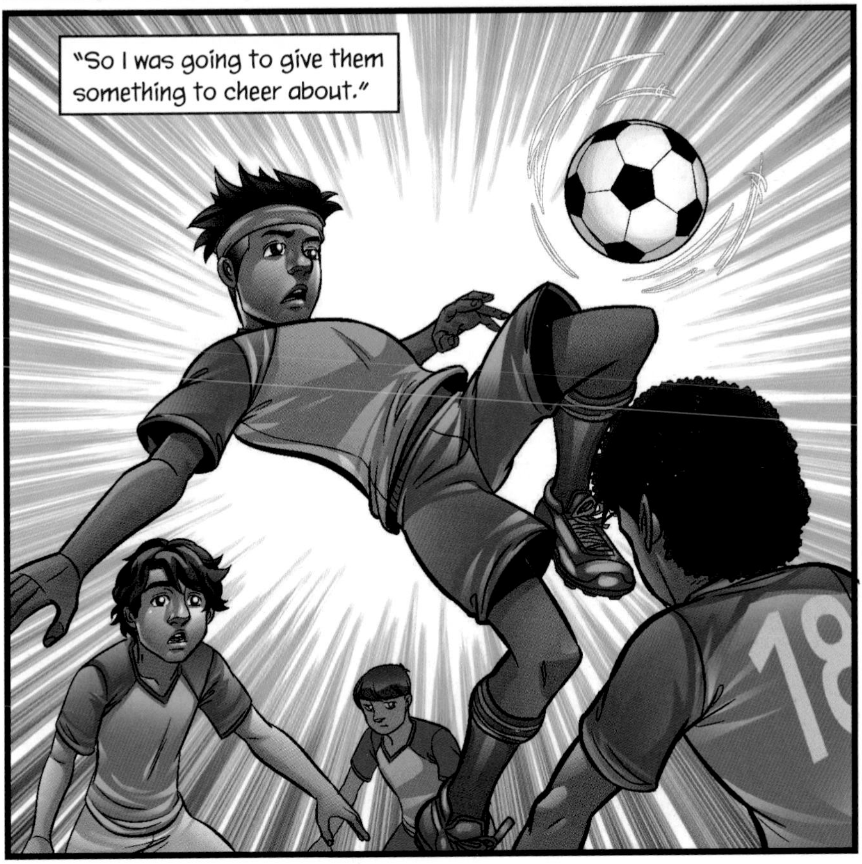
"So I was going to give them something to cheer about."
18

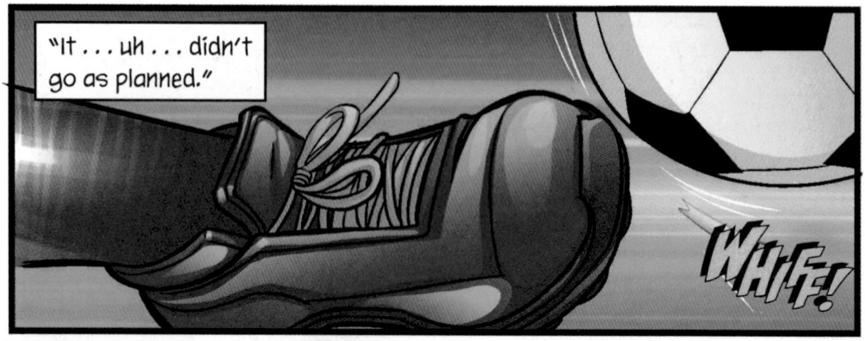
"It . . . uh . . . didn't go as planned."
WHIFF!

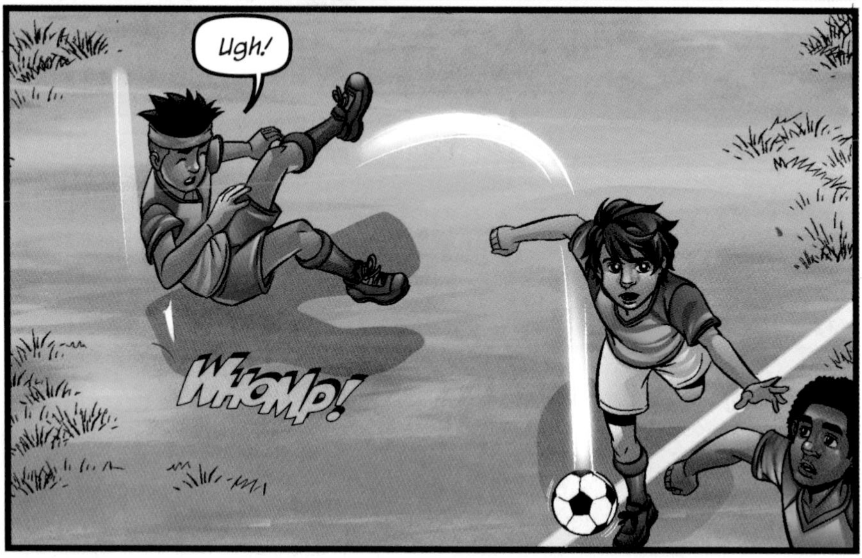
Ugh!
WHOMP!

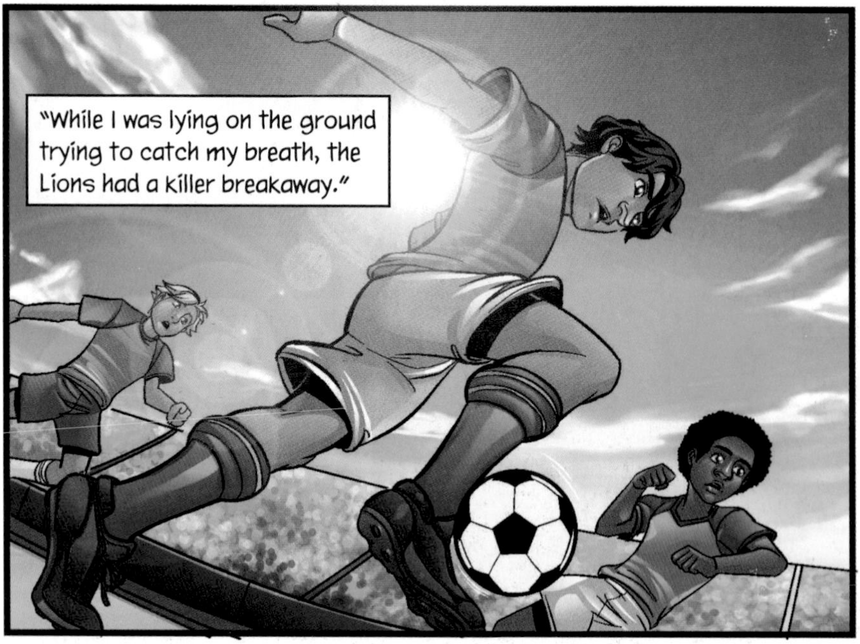
"While I was lying on the ground trying to catch my breath, the Lions had a killer breakaway."

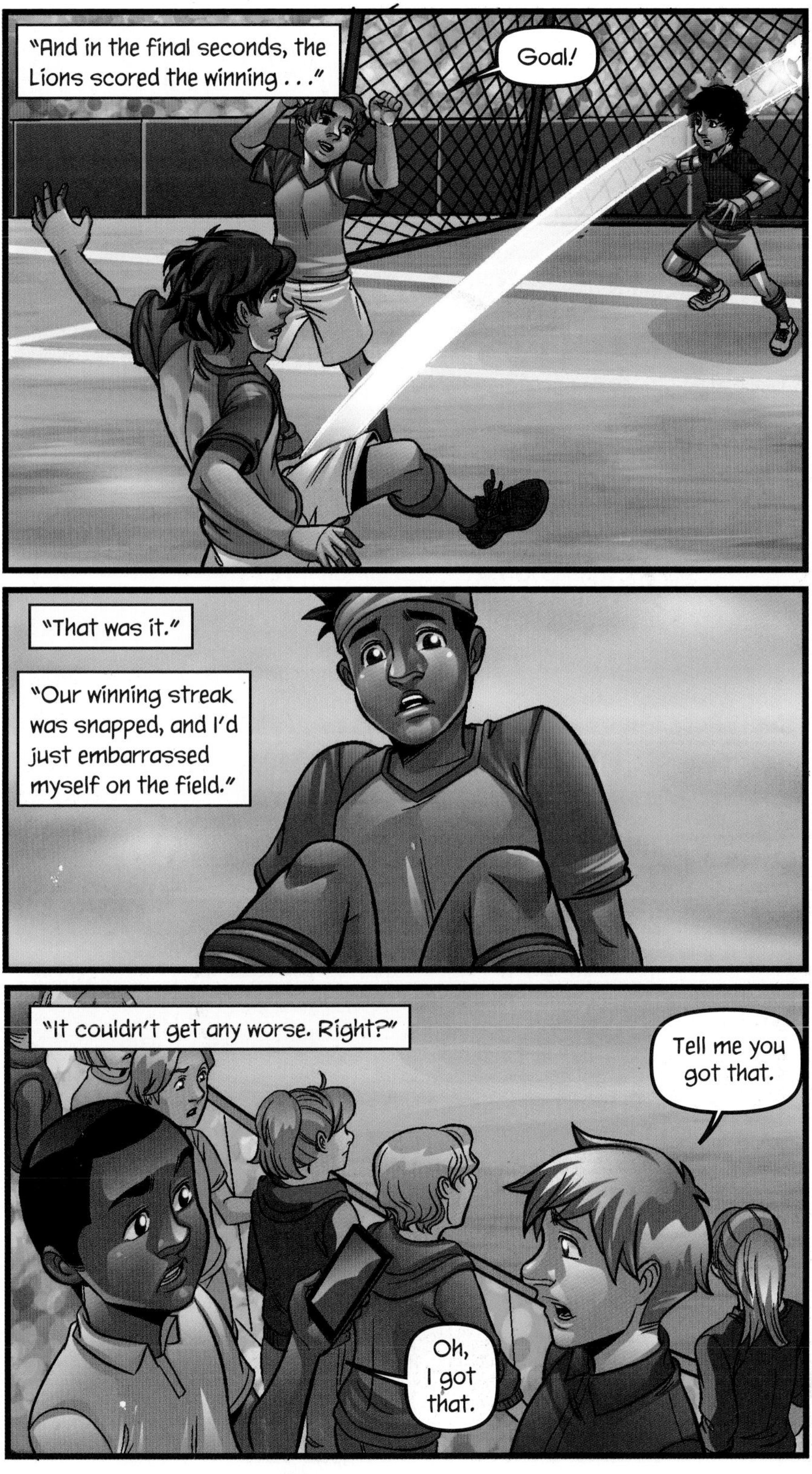
"And in the final seconds, the Lions scored the winning . . ."
Goal!
"That was it."
"Our winning streak was snapped, and I'd just embarrassed myself on the field."
"It couldn't get any worse. Right?"
Tell me you got that.
Oh, I got that.

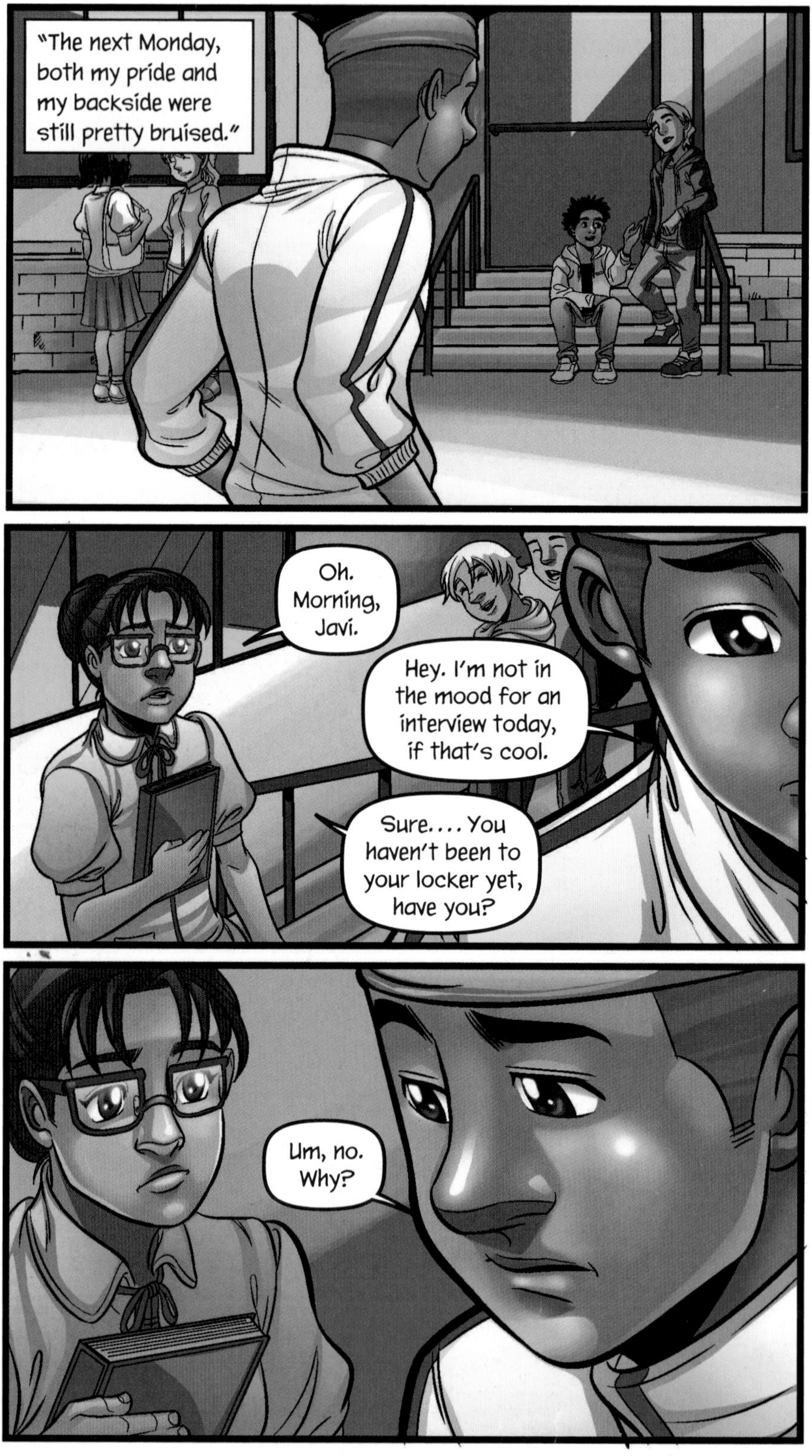
"The next Monday, both my pride and my backside were still pretty bruised."
Oh. Morning, Javi.
Hey. I'm not in the mood for an interview today, if that's cool.
Sure. . . . You haven't been to your locker yet, have you?
Um, no. Why?

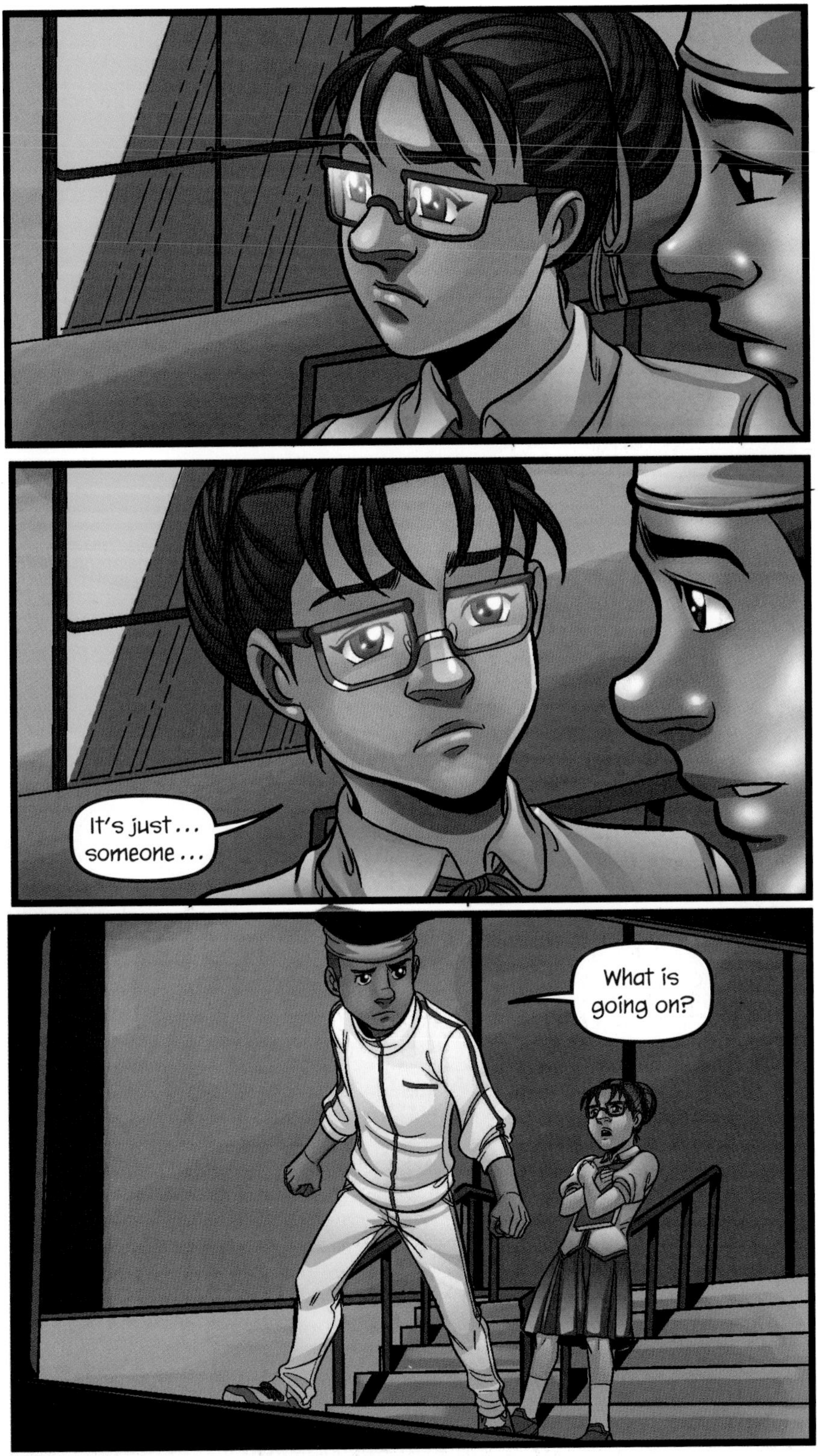
It's just...
someone...
What is
going on?

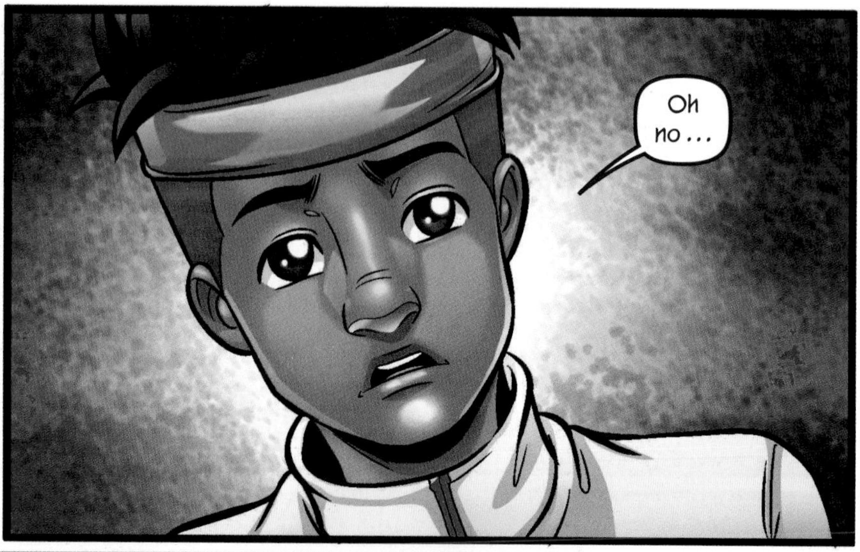
Oh no . . .

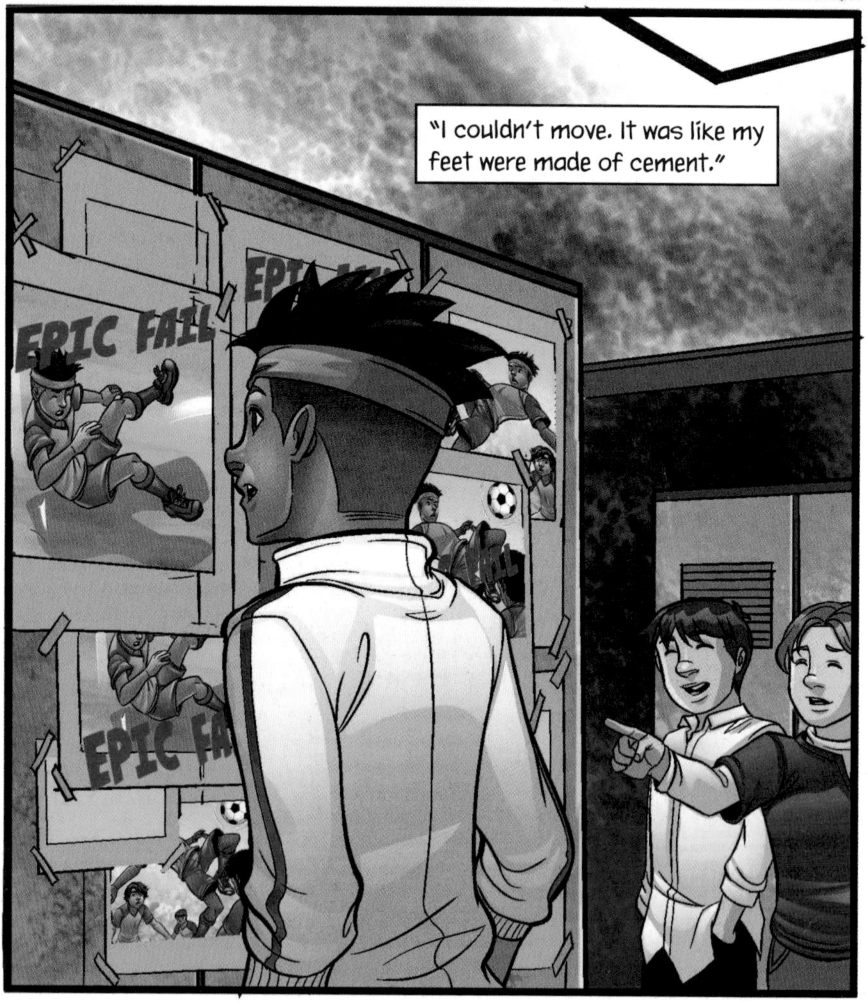
"I couldn't move. It was like my feet were made of cement."
EPIC FAIL
EPIC FAIL

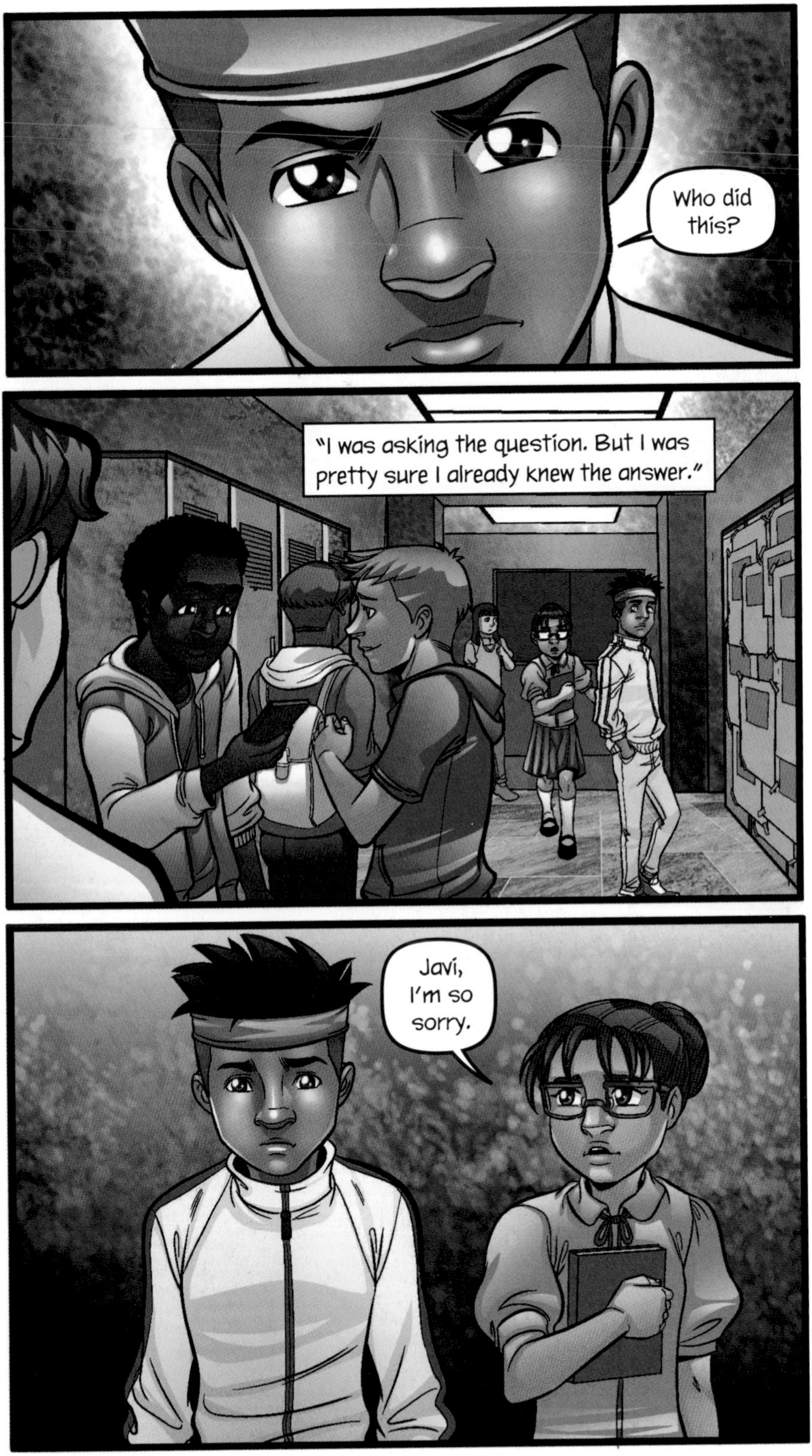
Who did this?
"I was asking the question. But I was pretty sure I already knew the answer."
Javi, I'm so sorry.

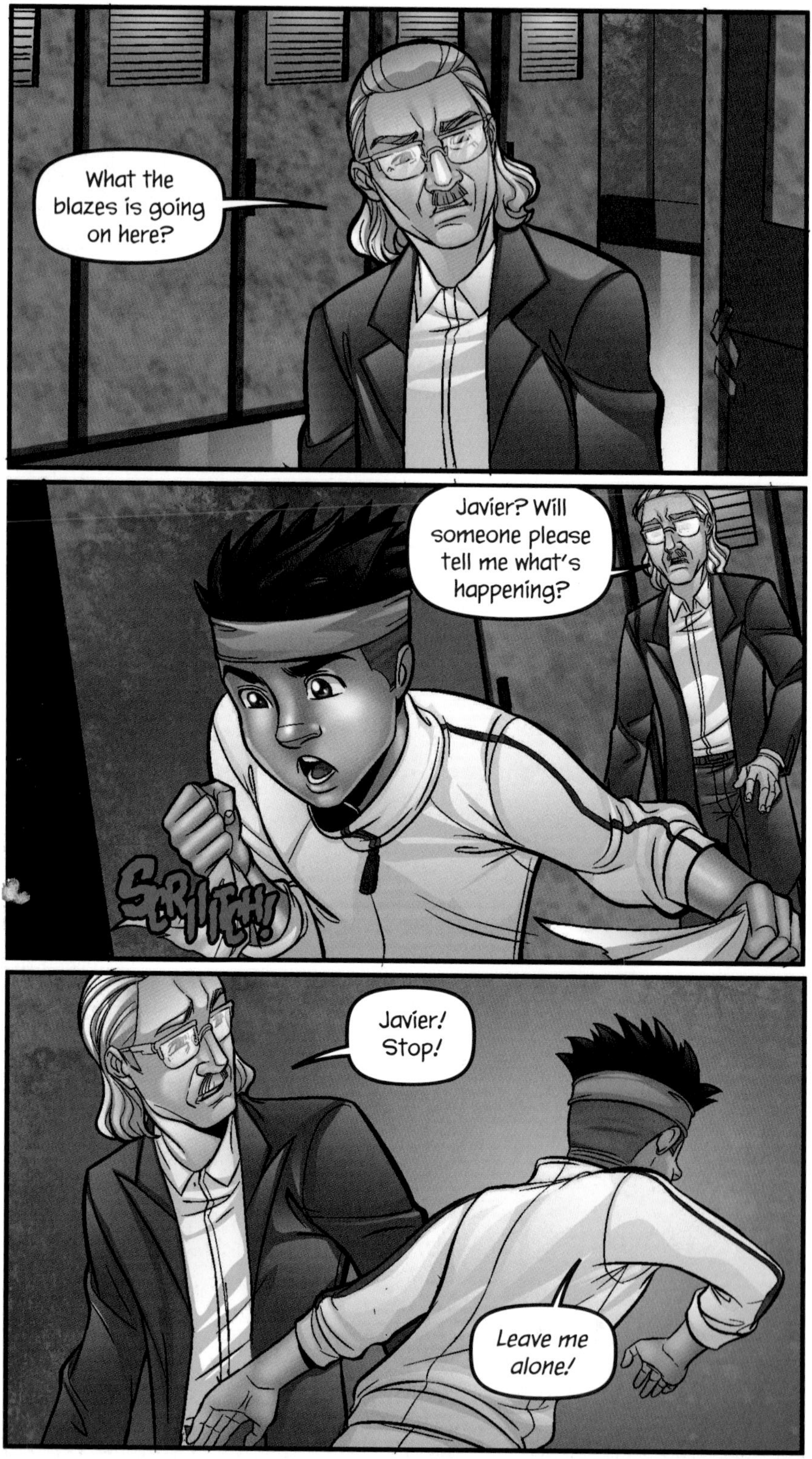
What the blazes is going on here?
Javier? Will someone please tell me what's happening?
SCRIIITCH!
Javier! Stop!
Leave me alone!

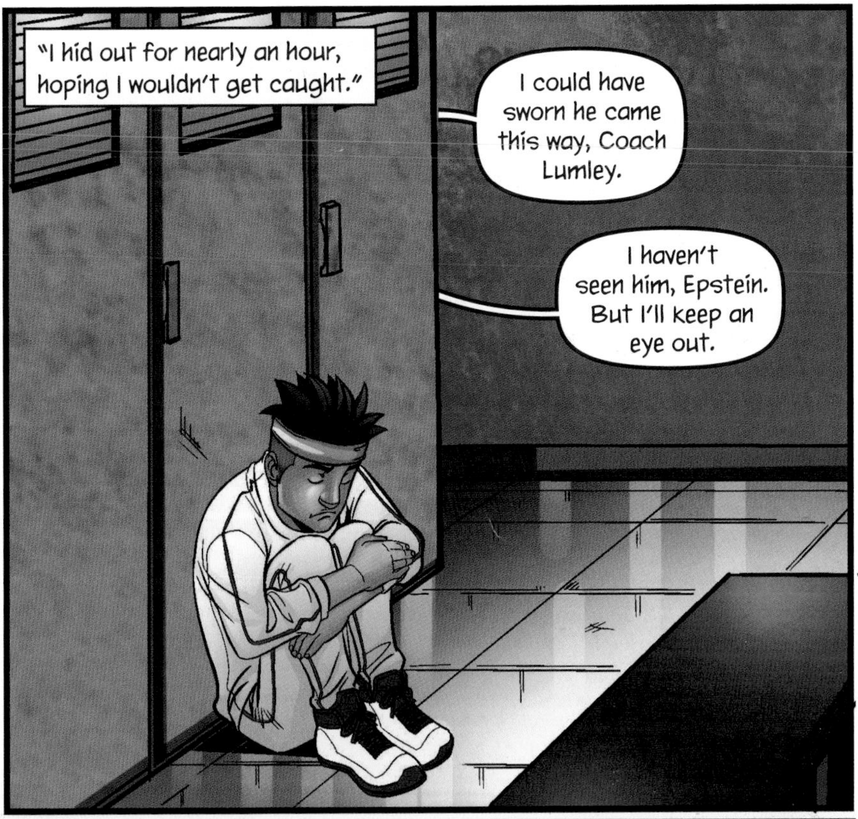
"I hid out for nearly an hour, hoping I wouldn't get caught."
I could have sworn he came this way, Coach Lumley.
I haven't seen him, Epstein. But I'll keep an eye out.

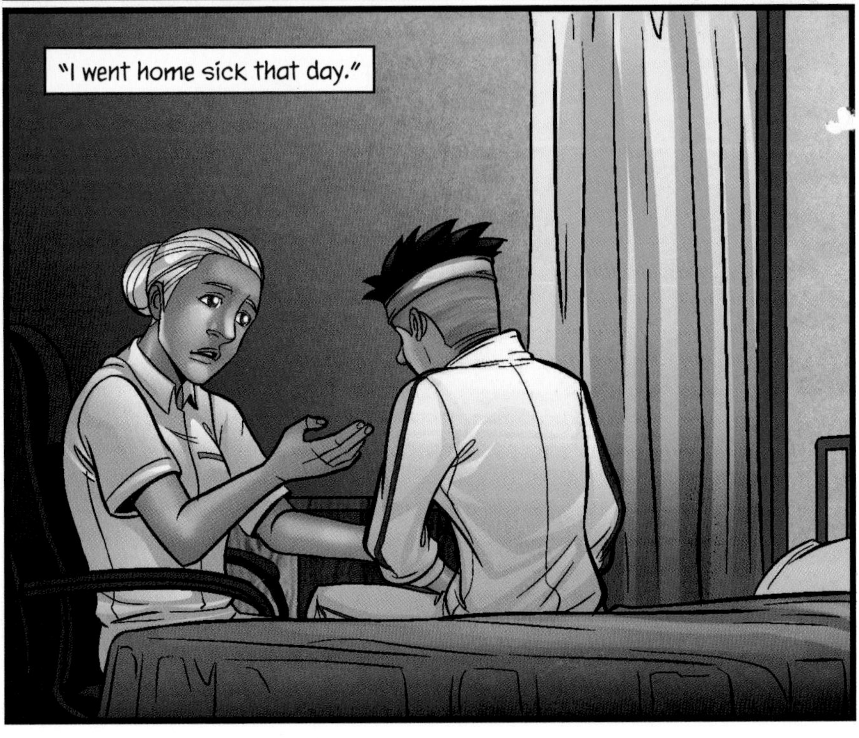
"I went home sick that day."

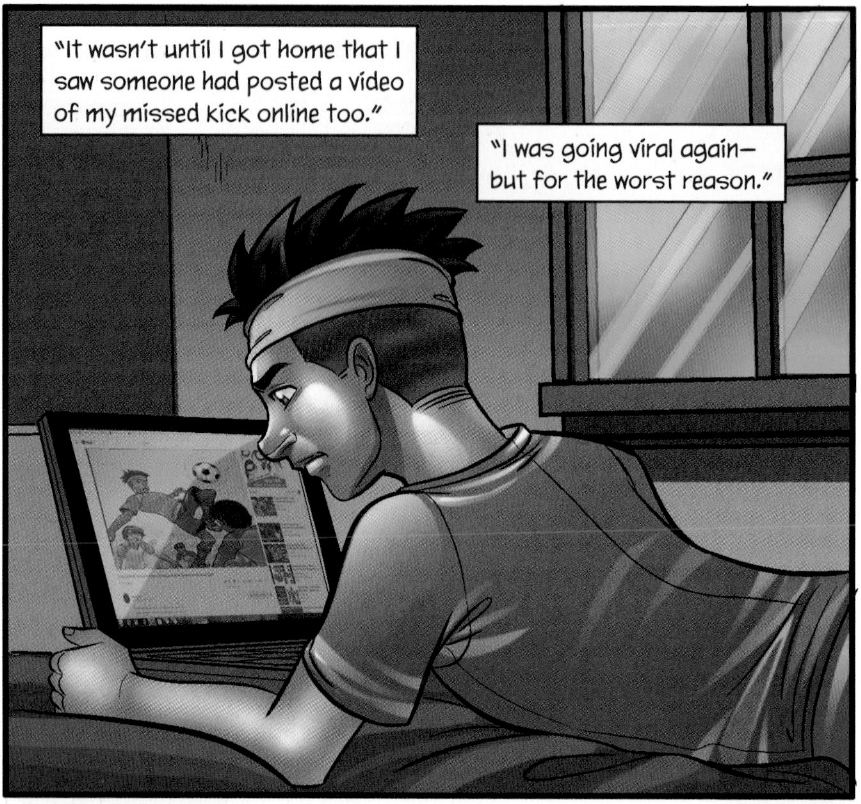
"It wasn't until I got home that I saw someone had posted a video of my missed kick online too."
"I was going viral again—but for the worst reason."

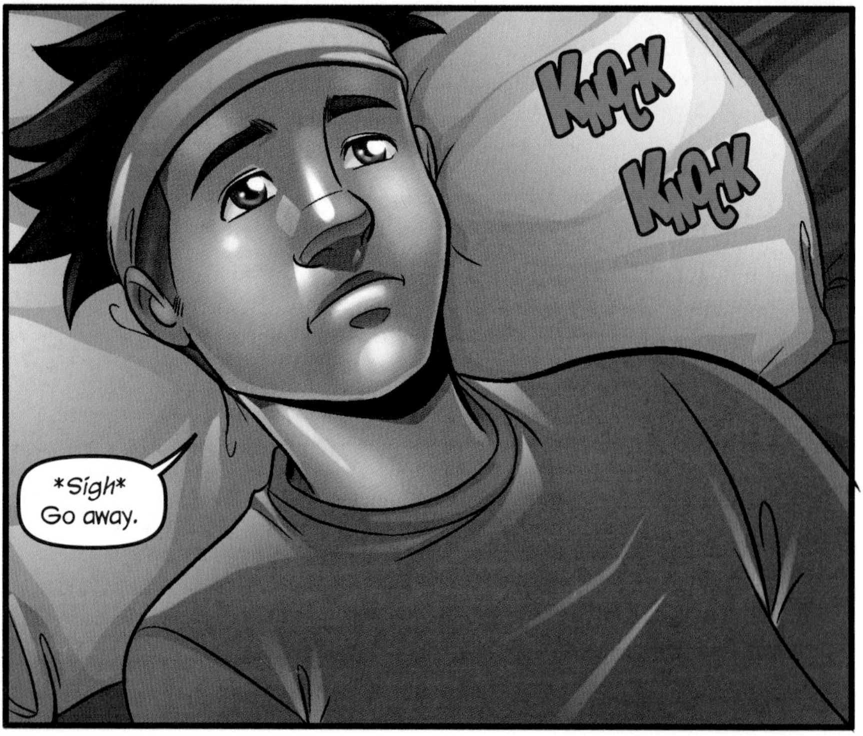
KNOCK
KNOCK
Sigh Go away.

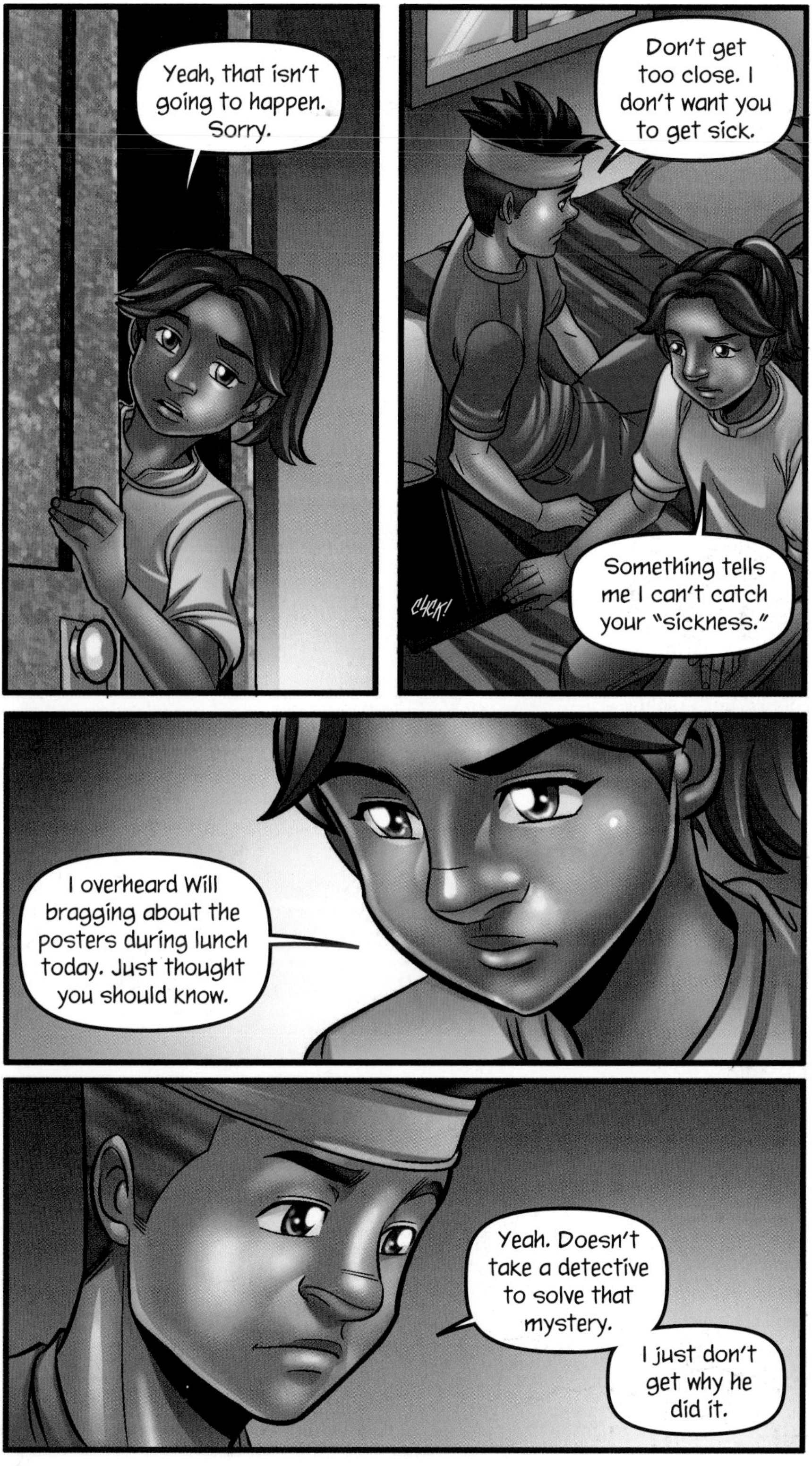
Yeah, that isn't going to happen. Sorry.
Don't get too close. I don't want you to get sick.
CHCK!
Something tells me I can't catch your "sickness."
I overheard Will bragging about the posters during lunch today. Just thought you should know.
Yeah. Doesn't take a detective to solve that mystery.
I just don't get why he did it.

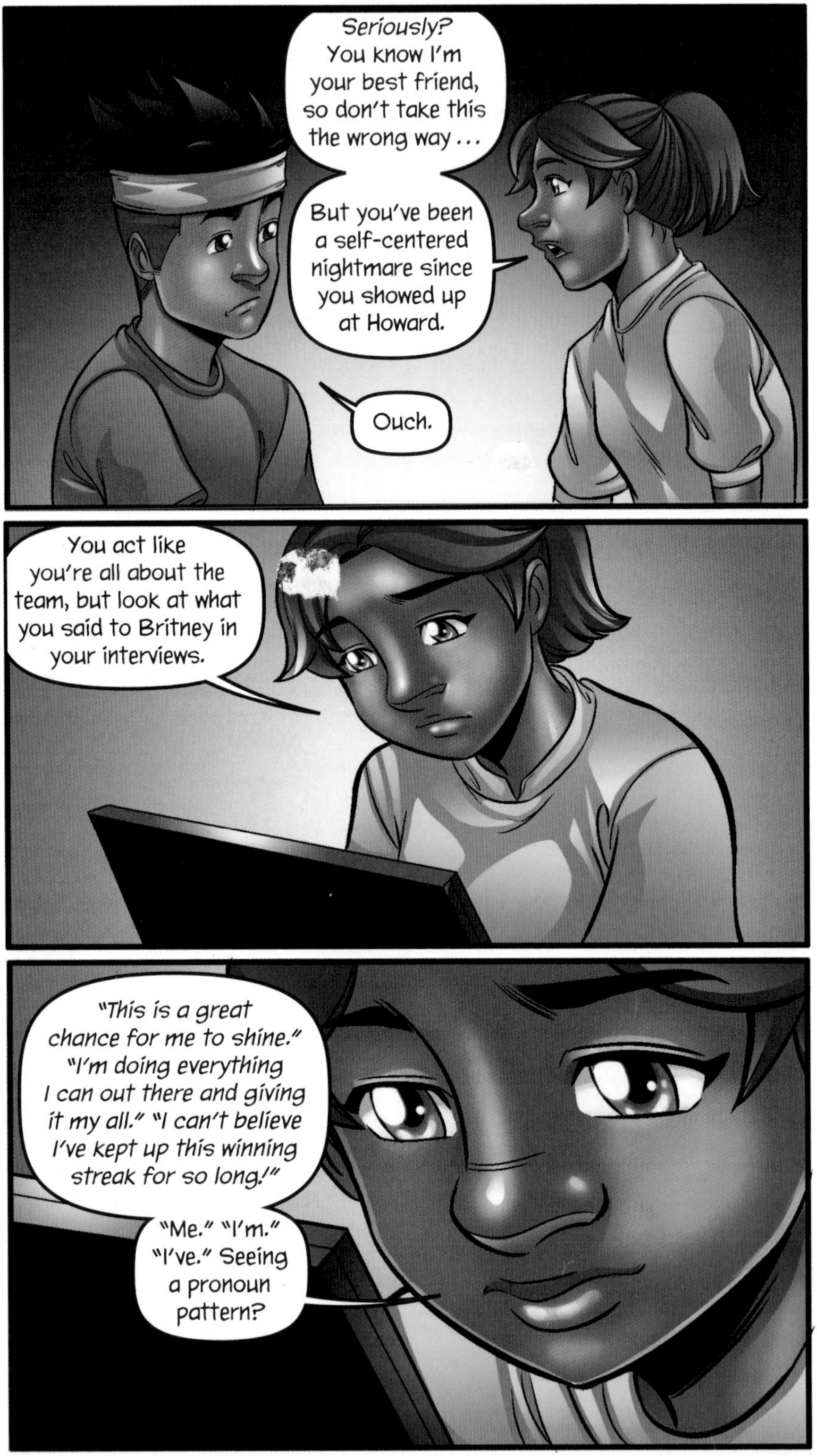
Seriously? You know I'm your best friend, so don't take this the wrong way . . .
But you've been a self-centered nightmare since you showed up at Howard.
Ouch.
You act like you're all about the team, but look at what you said to Britney in your interviews.
"This is a great chance for me to shine." "I'm doing everything I can out there and giving it my all." "I can't believe I've kept up this winning streak for so long!"
"Me." "I'm." "I've." Seeing a pronoun pattern?

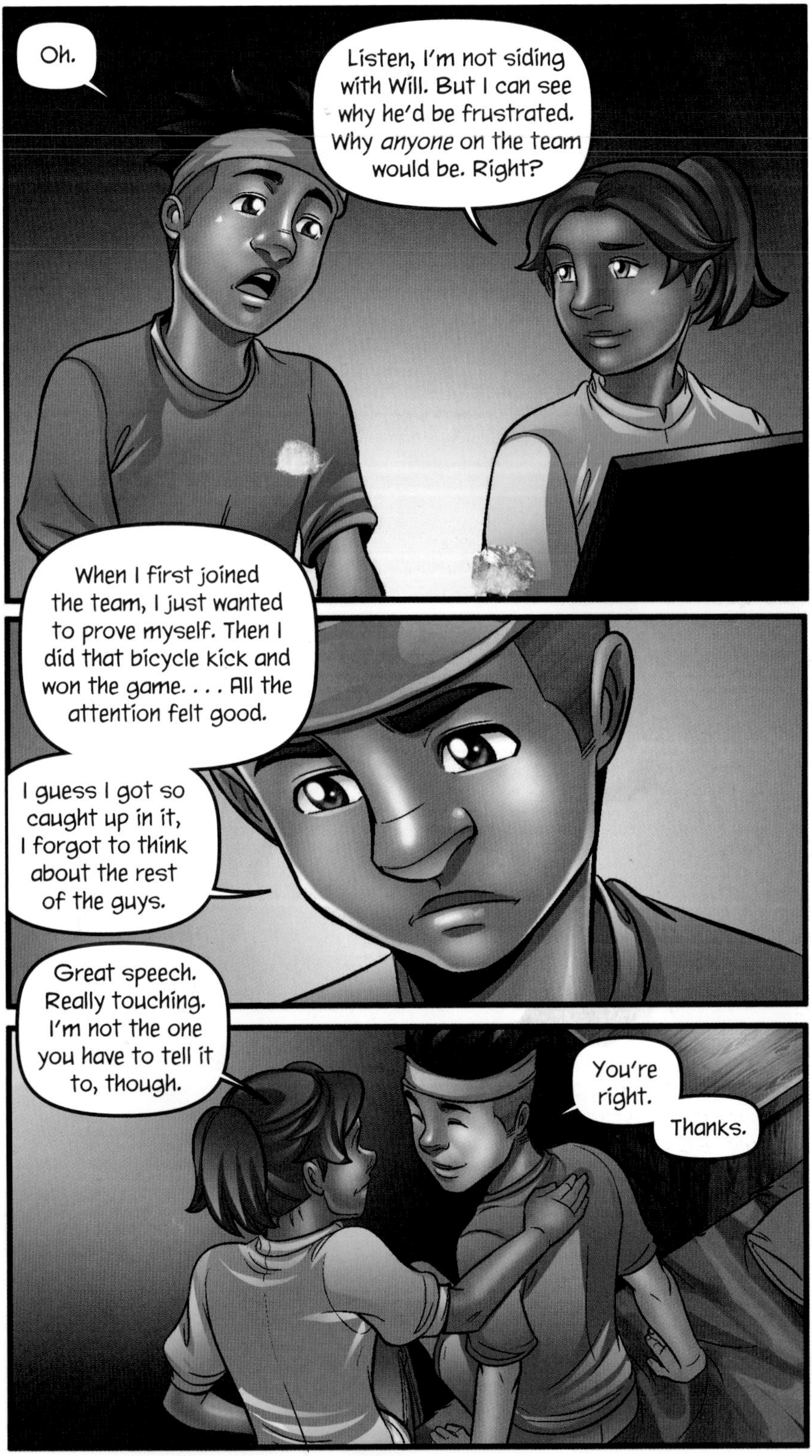
Oh.
Listen, I'm not siding with Will. But I can see why he'd be frustrated. Why *anyone* on the team would be. Right?
When I first joined the team, I just wanted to prove myself. Then I did that bicycle kick and won the game. . . . All the attention felt good.
I guess I got so caught up in it, I forgot to think about the rest of the guys.
Great speech. Really touching. I'm not the one you have to tell it to, though.
You're right.
Thanks.

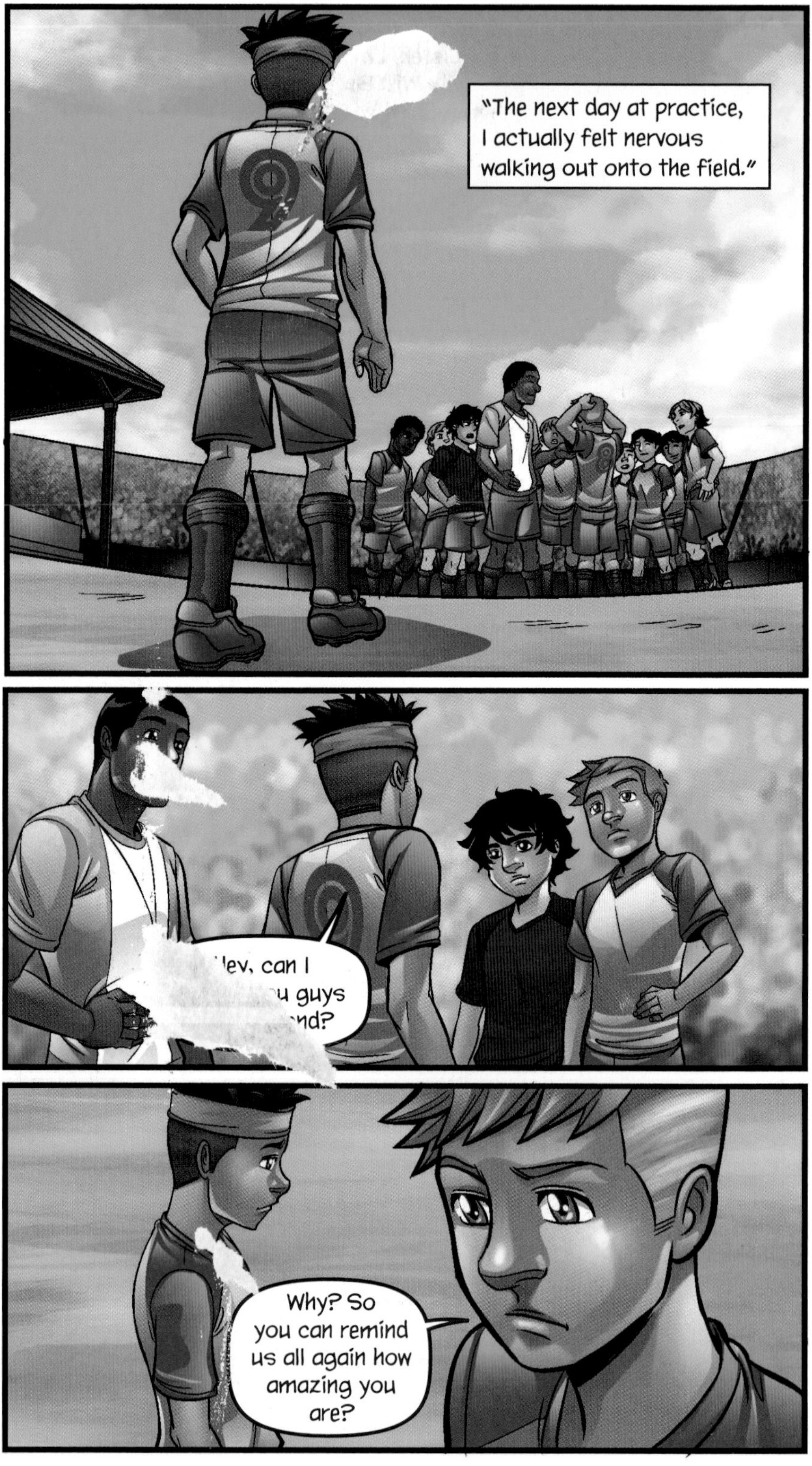
"The next day at practice, I actually felt nervous walking out onto the field."
lev, can I
u guys
nd?
Why? So you can remind us all again how amazing you are?

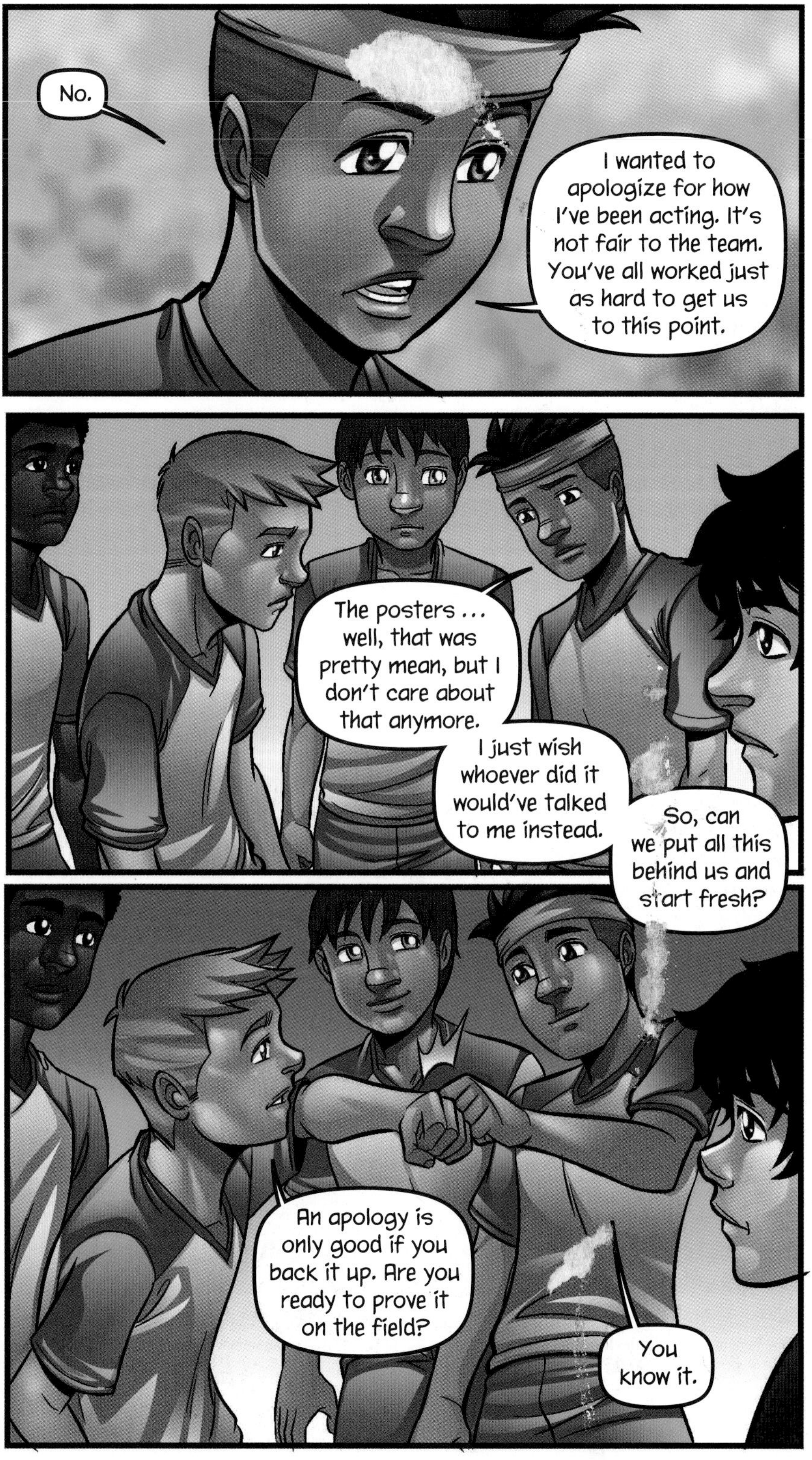
No.
I wanted to apologize for how I've been acting. It's not fair to the team. You've all worked just as hard to get us to this point.
The posters ... well, that was pretty mean, but I don't care about that anymore.
I just wish whoever did it would've talked to me instead.
So, can we put all this behind us and start fresh?
An apology is only good if you back it up. Are you ready to prove it on the field?
You know it.

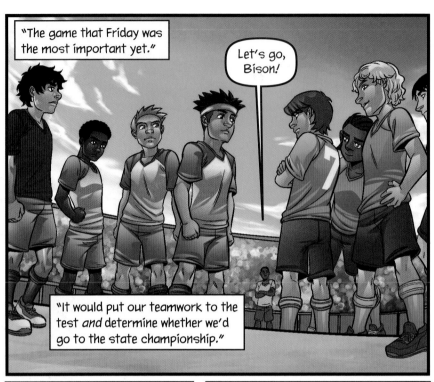

"The game that Friday was the most important yet."

Let's go, Bison!

"It would put our teamwork to the test *and* determine whether we'd go to the state championship."

"The Scorpions meant business. And apparently they had done their homework on us."

Gonna have another one of your "epic fails"?

THWUMP!

"I was caught off guard. In that split second, the Scorpion snatched the ball. He passed it downfield . . ."

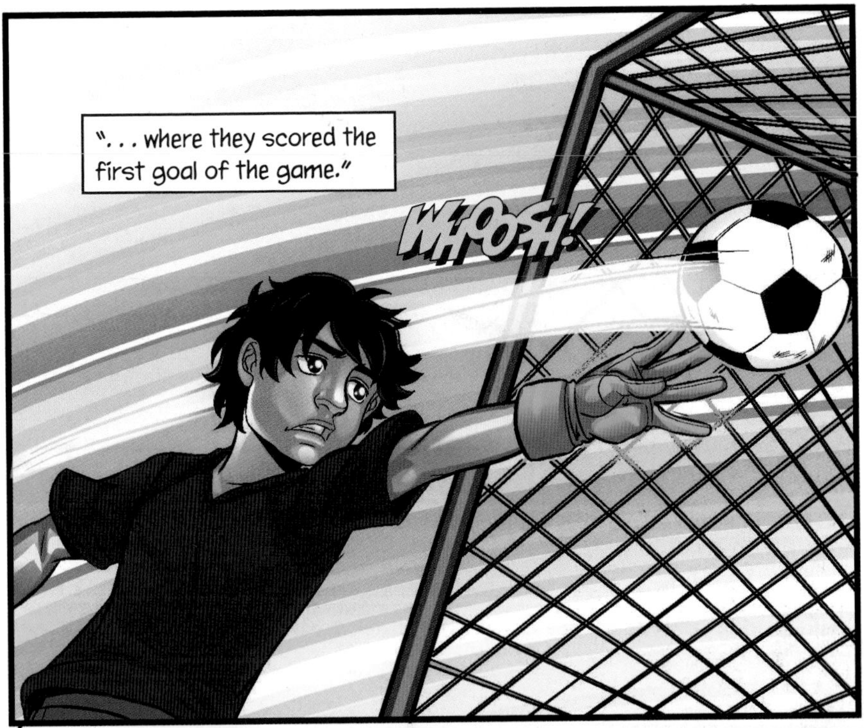
". . . where they scored the first goal of the game."
WHOOSH!

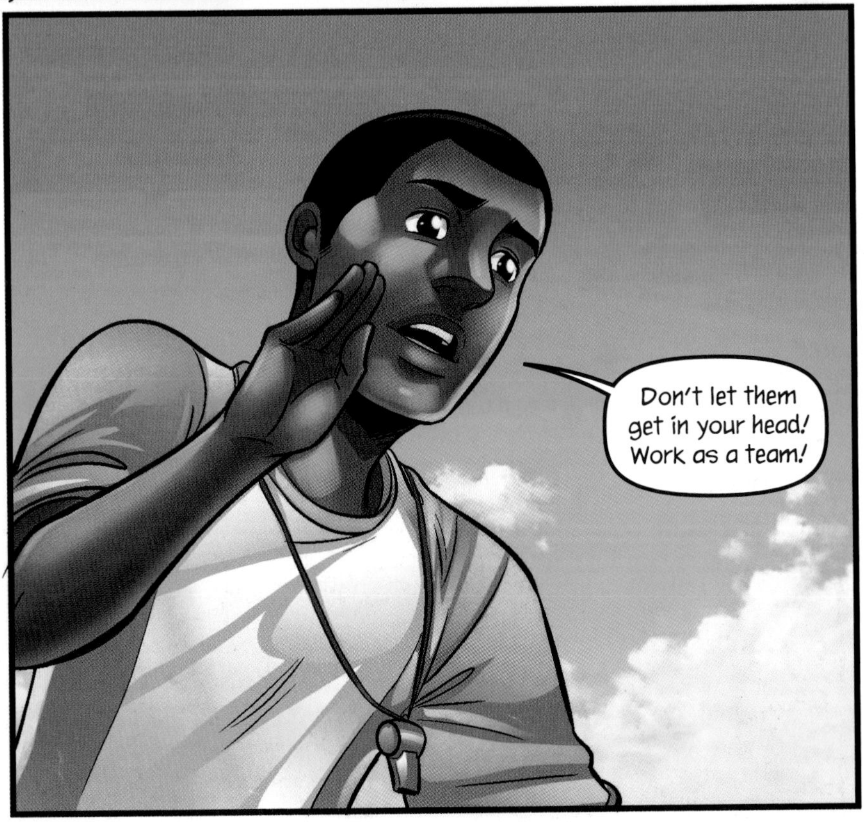
Don't let them get in your head! Work as a team!

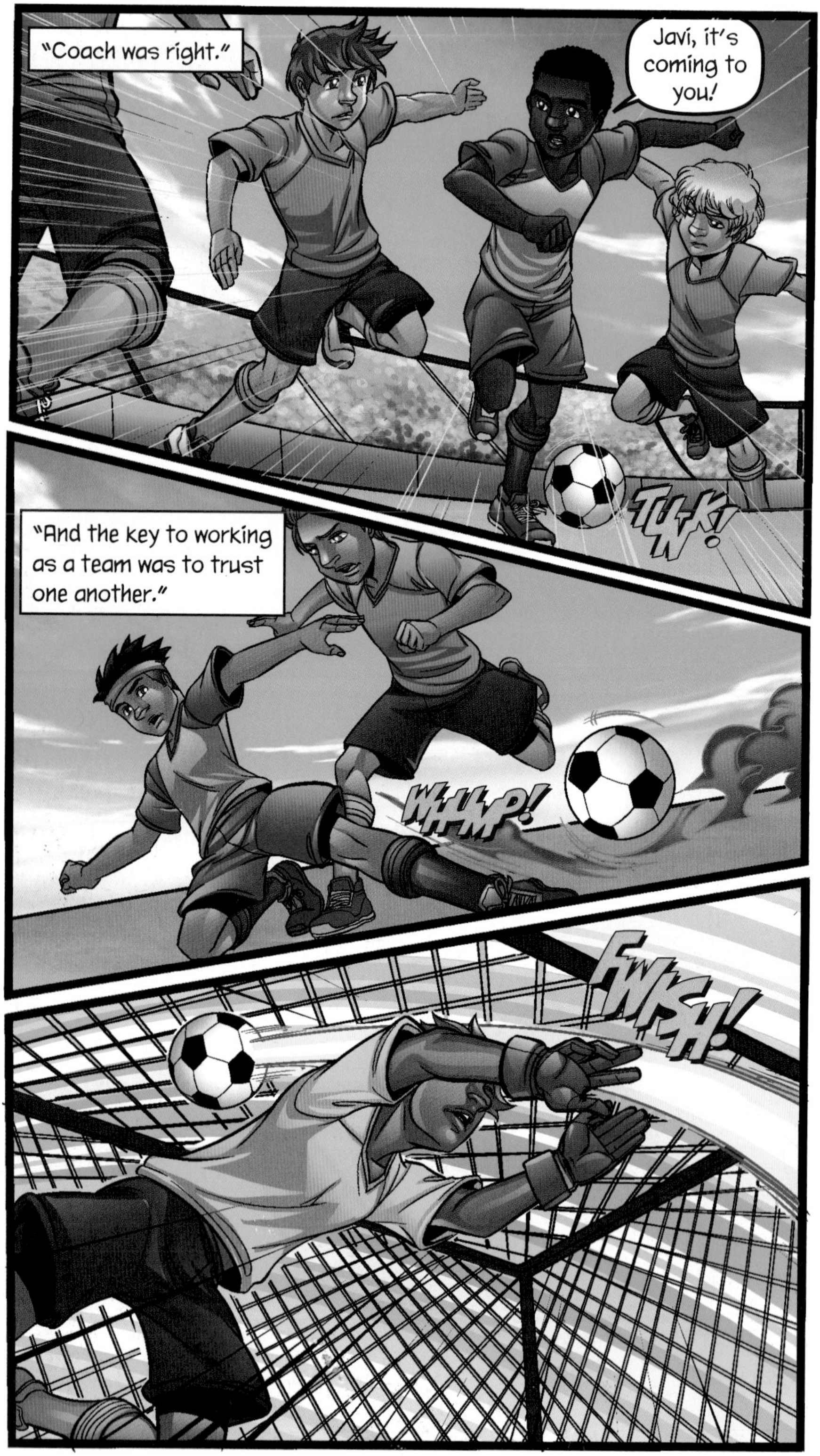
"Coach was right."
Javi, it's coming to you!
TUK!
"And the key to working as a team was to trust one another."
WHUMP!
FWISH!

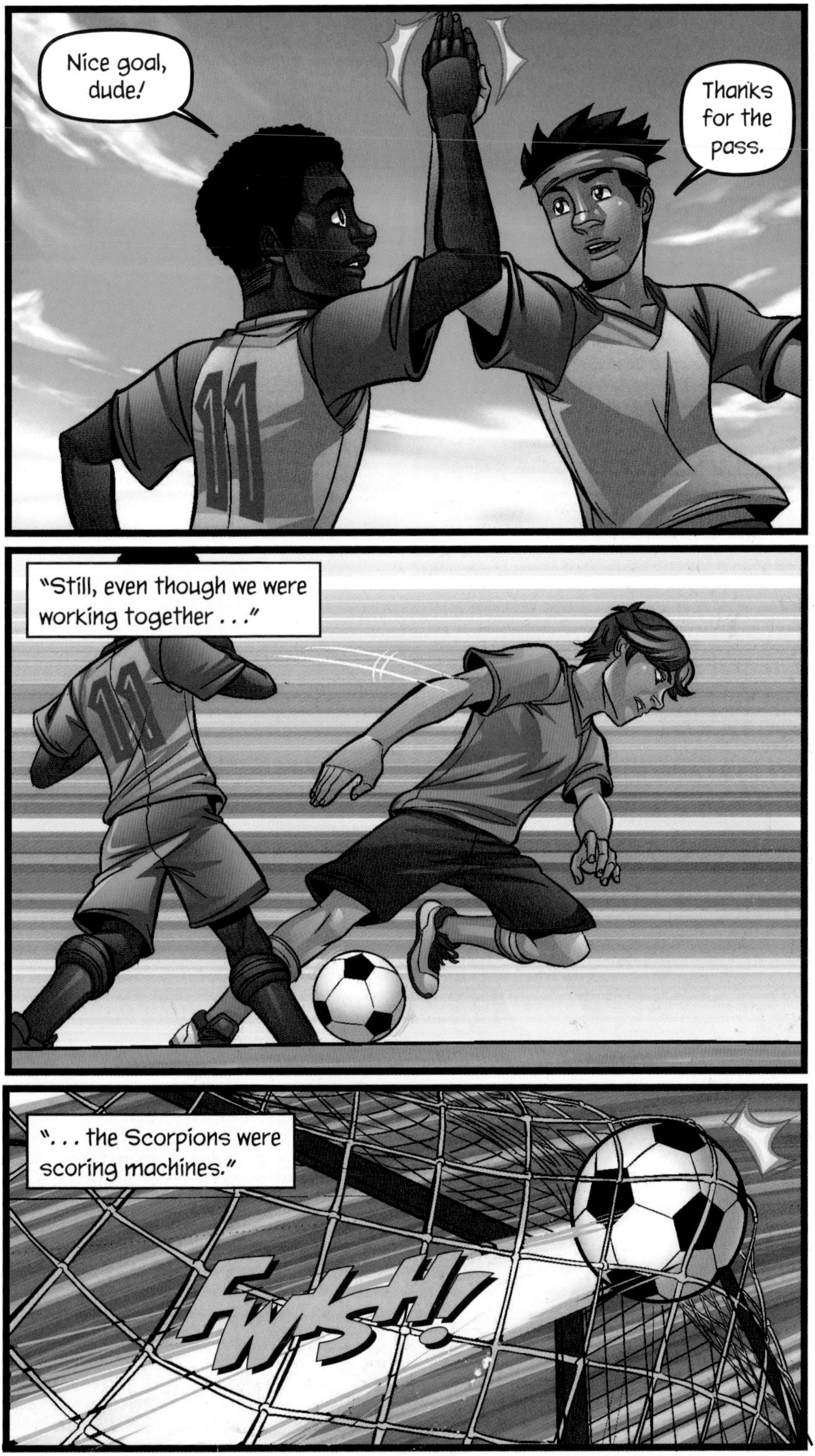
Nice goal, dude!
Thanks for the pass.
"Still, even though we were working together . . ."
". . . the Scorpions were scoring machines."
FWISH!

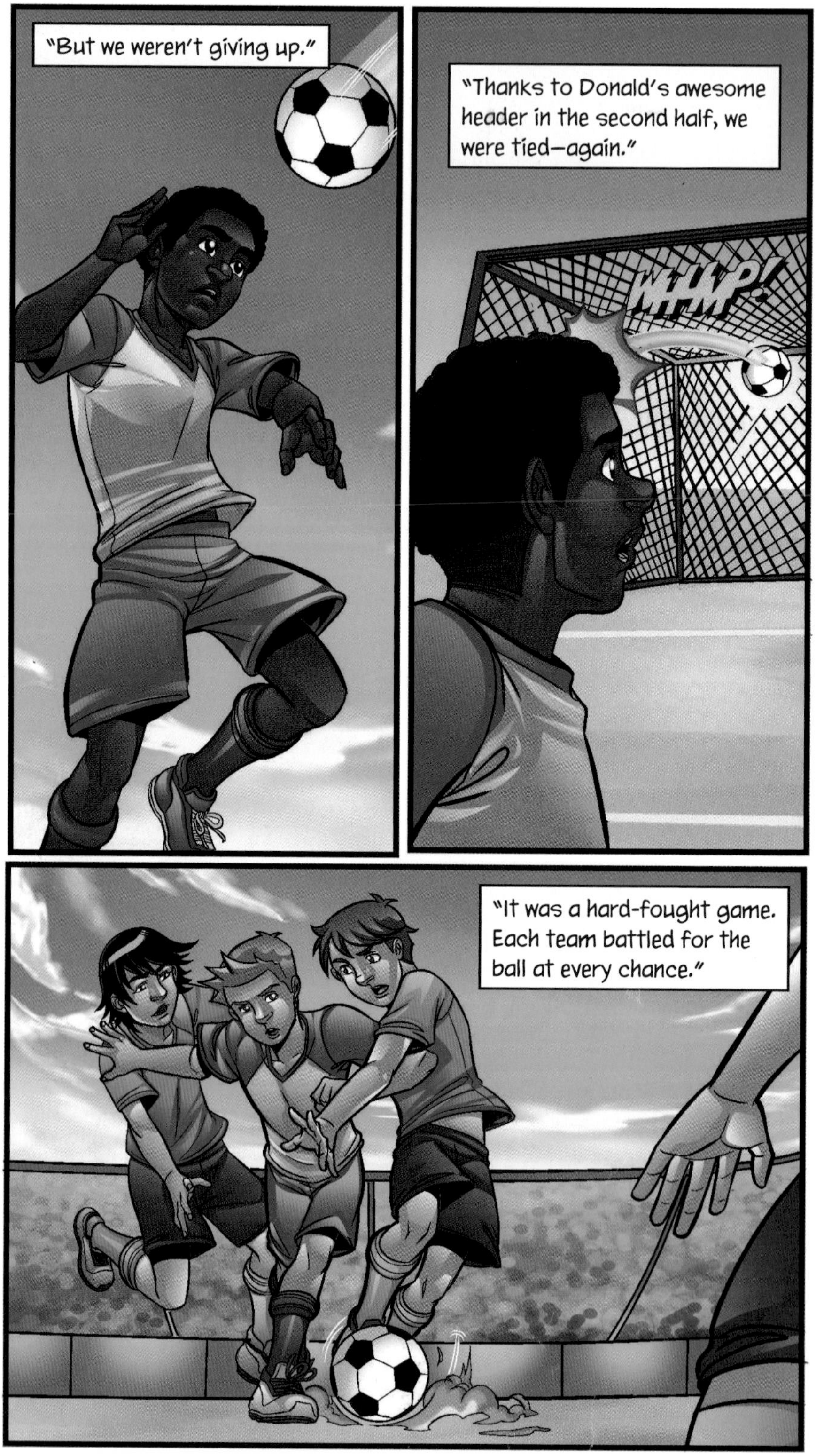
"But we weren't giving up."
"Thanks to Donald's awesome header in the second half, we were tied—again."
WHUMP!
"It was a hard-fought game. Each team battled for the ball at every chance."

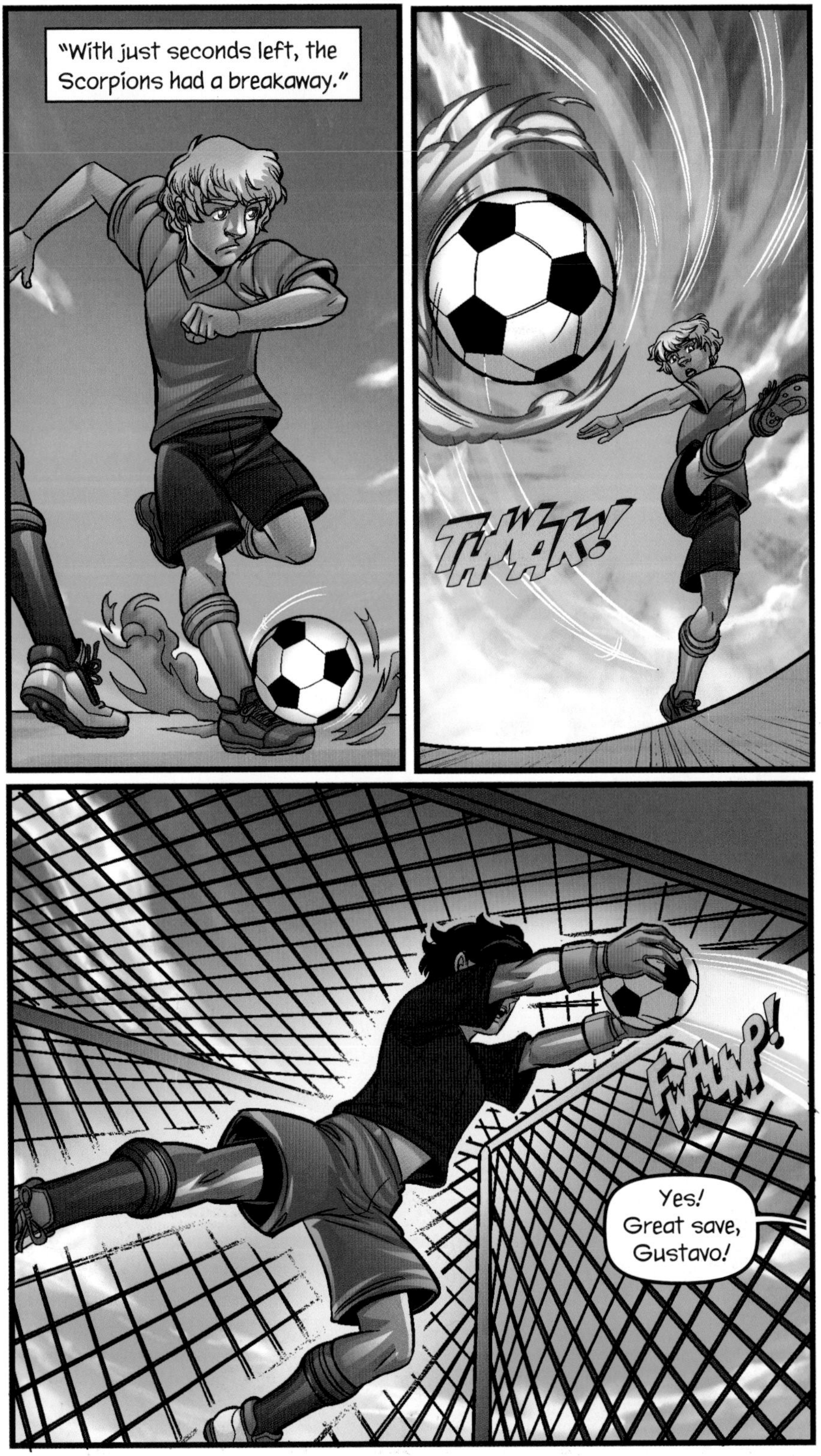
"With just seconds left, the Scorpions had a breakaway."
THWAK!
FWHUMP!
Yes! Great save, Gustavo!

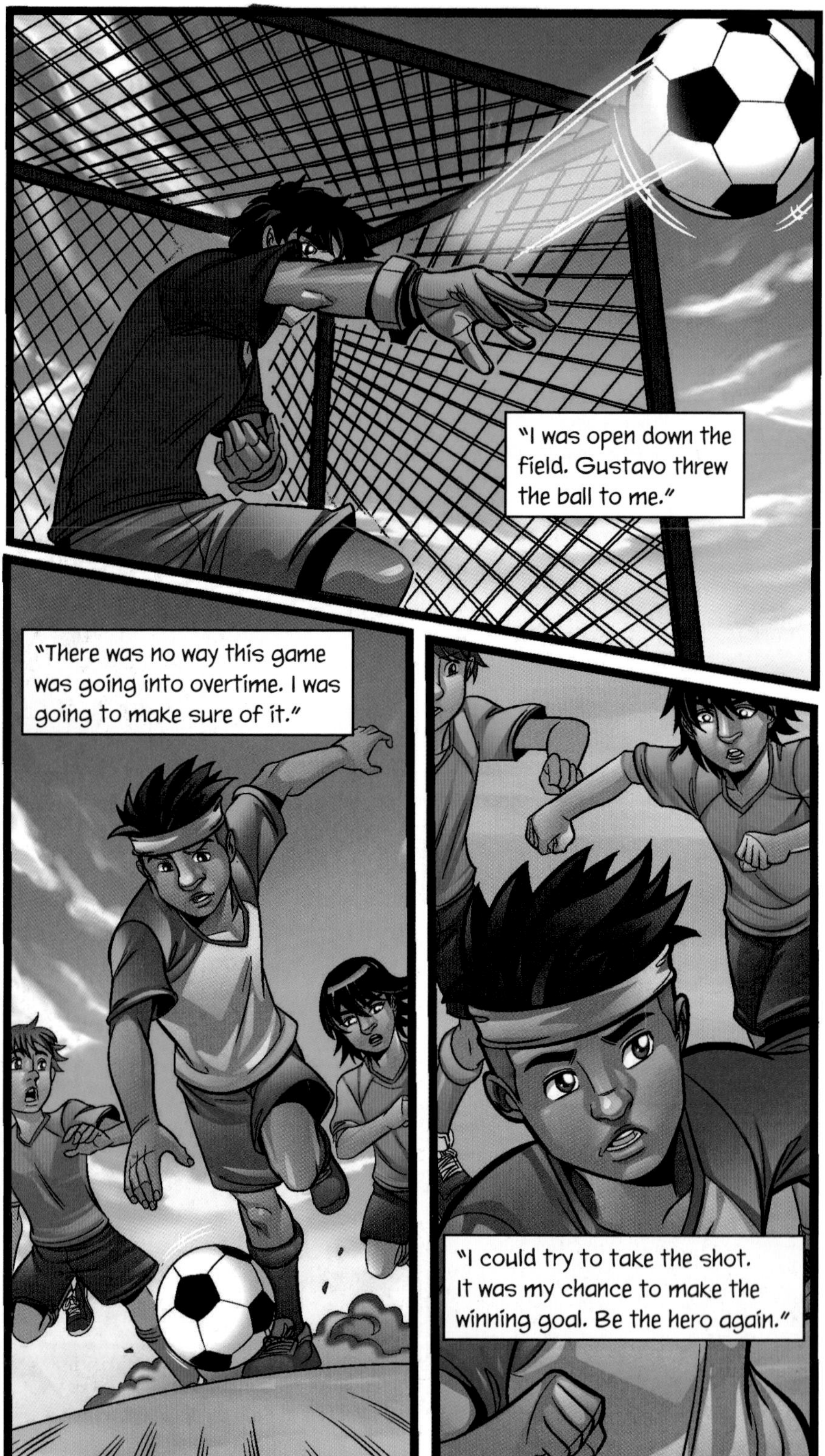
"I was open down the field. Gustavo threw the ball to me."
"There was no way this game was going into overtime. I was going to make sure of it."
"I could try to take the shot. It was my chance to make the winning goal. Be the hero again."

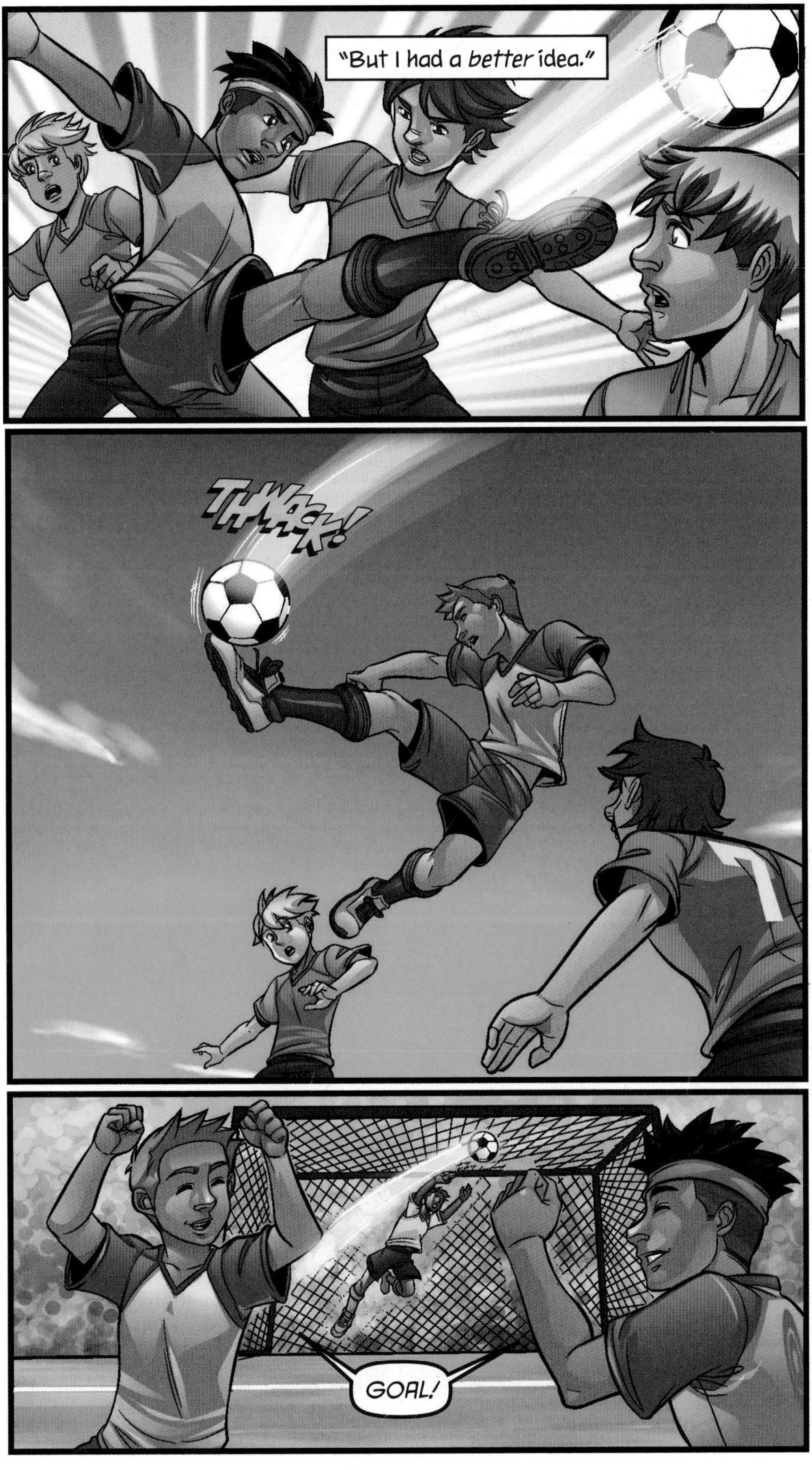
"But I had a *better* idea."
THWACK!
GOAL!

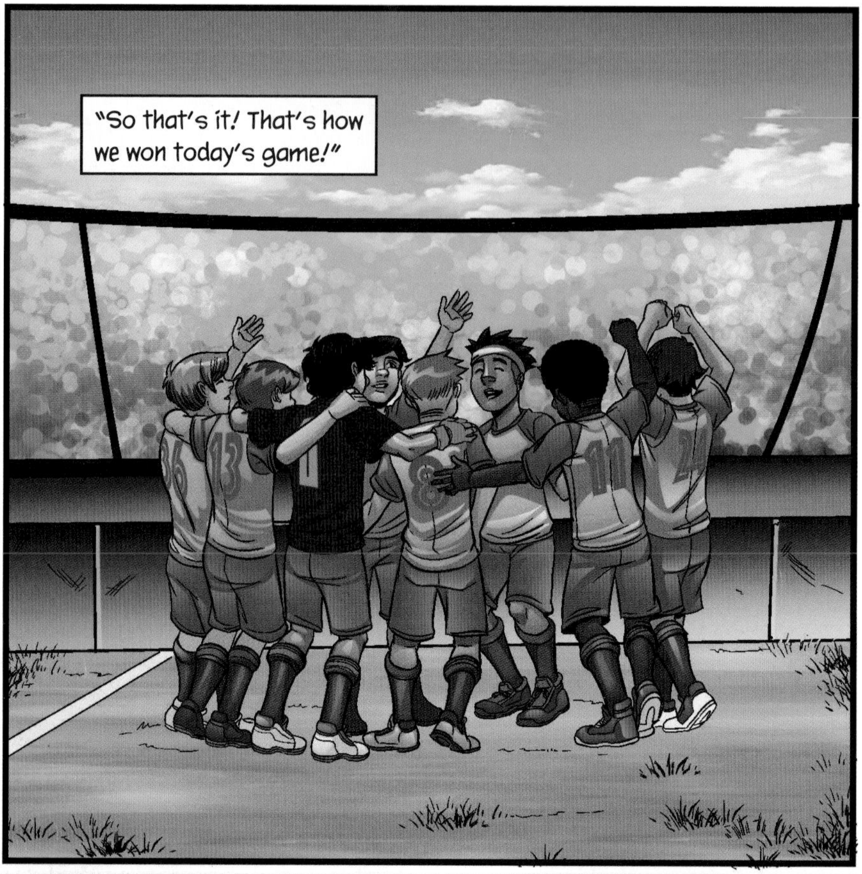
"So that's it! That's how we won today's game!"
36
13
1
8
11
24

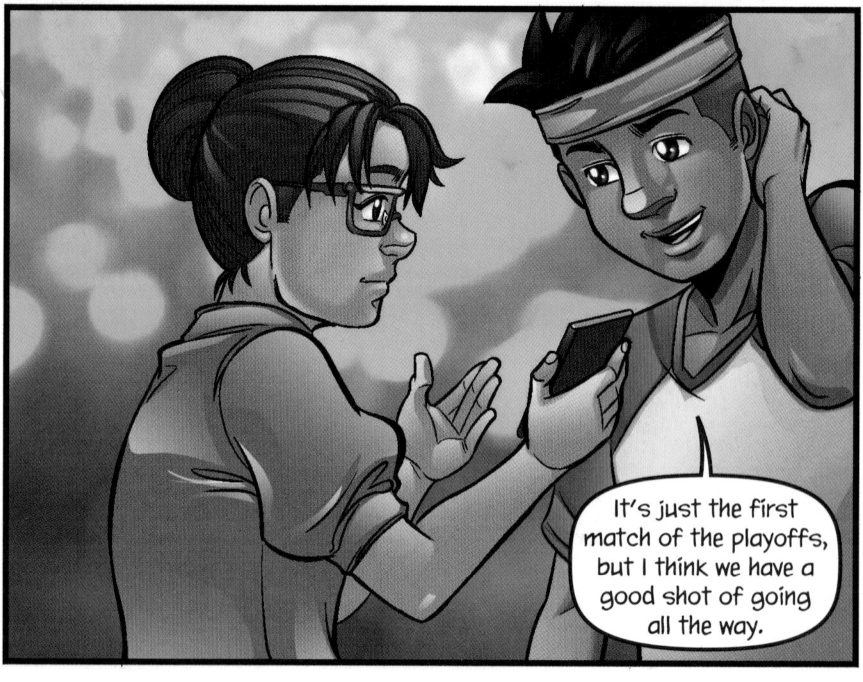
It's just the first match of the playoffs, but I think we have a good shot of going all the way.

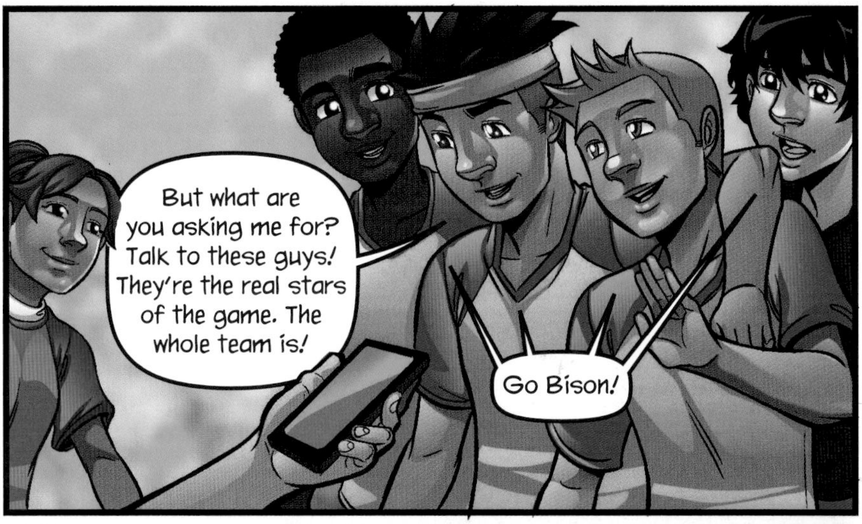
But what are you asking me for? Talk to these guys! They're the real stars of the game. The whole team is!
Go Bison!

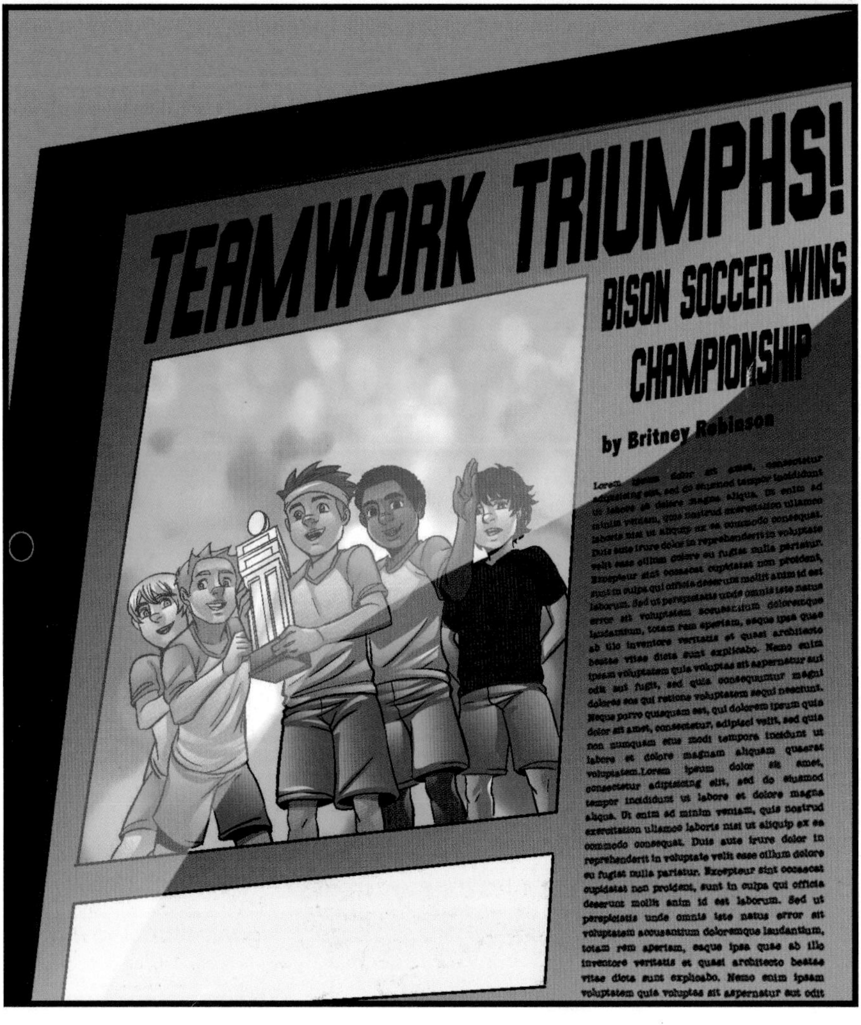
TEAMWORK TRIUMPHS!
BISON SOCCER WINS CHAMPIONSHIP
by Britney Robinson

VISUAL QUESTIONS

1. Javi says that the team has his back. Look at the art. Do you think what Javi says is true? Why or why not?

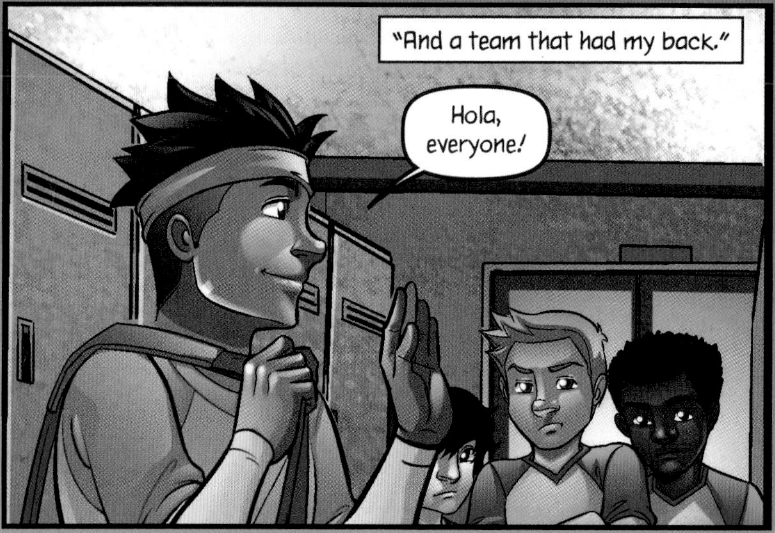
"And a team that had my back."
Hola, everyone!

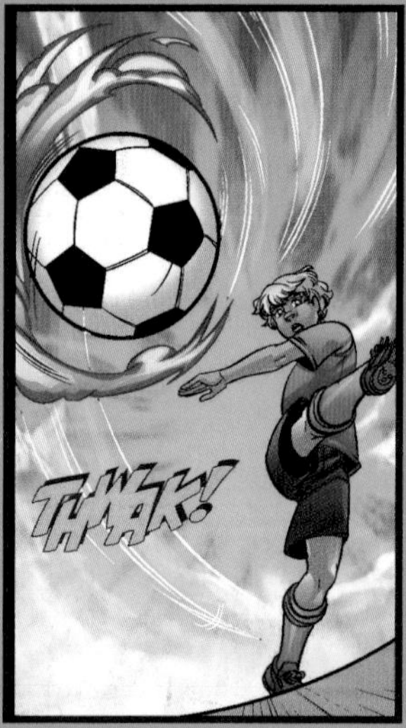
THWAK!

2. The soccer ball isn't actually on fire. So why do you think the artist put flames circling around it?

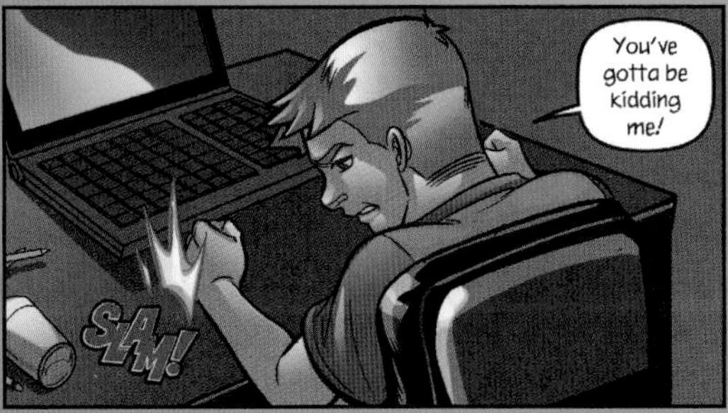
You've gotta be kidding me!
SLAM!

3. Together, the art and text in comics can give you a lot of information. How does Will feel here from page 31? Why does he feel that way?

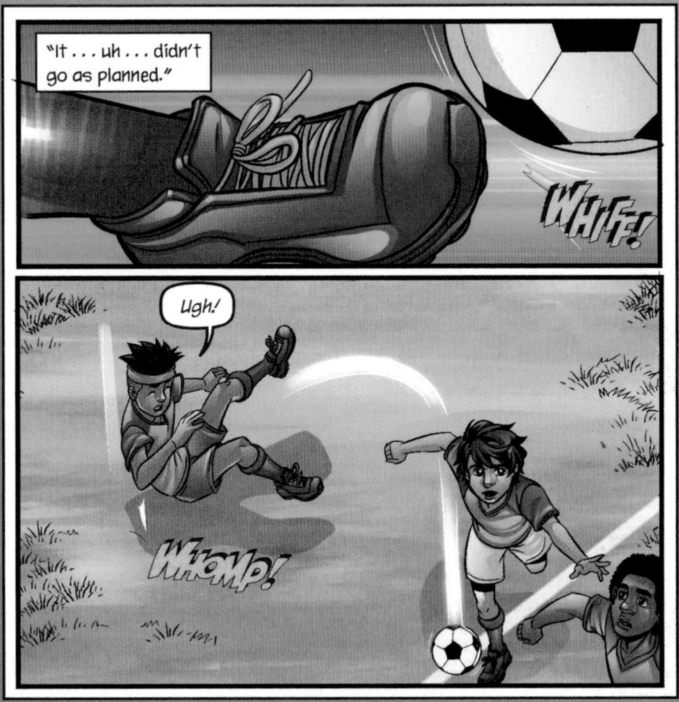
"It . . . uh . . . didn't go as planned."
WHIFF!
Ugh!
WHOMP!

4. Pretend you are the announcer for the Bisons' soccer game. Describe the action here and be sure to make it exciting! (Look at page 42 if you need a reminder.)

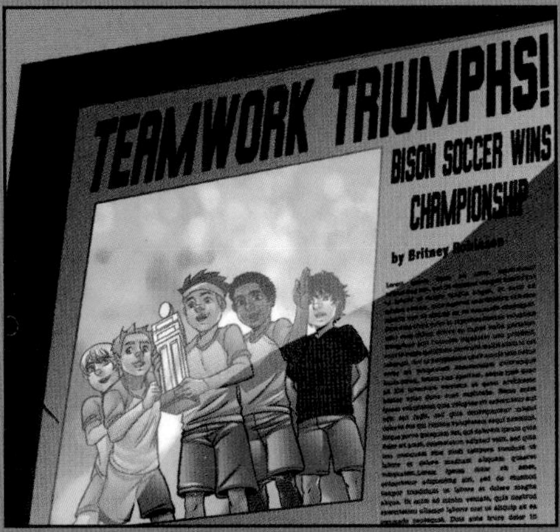
TEAMWORK TRIUMPHS!
BISON SOCCER WINS CHAMPIONSHIP
by Britney

5. Compare the first and last panels of the story. How are they the same and how are they different? In what ways does the final image show how Javi has changed?

SOCCER POSITIONS

Every soccer match begins with eleven players on each side of the field. Teammates work together to fight for the win. But what are the various positions, and what roles do they play? There are four basic position groupings that any soccer fan needs to know—read on to find out more!

Forwards
Midfielders
Defenders
Goalkeeper

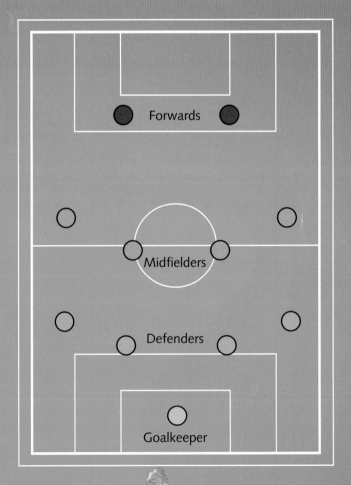

Forwards—These players focus on attacking and scoring as often as possible. They mostly stay on the other team's half of the field. Forwards look for opportunities to score, or they set up others to take the shot. In order to be successful, they must be quick and have great ball control. Forwards are sometimes called strikers, although some people only give that title to the team's main goal-maker. Forward positions can include: striker, second striker, center forward.

Midfielders—Like the name suggests, midfielders play in the middle of the field. They can attack or defend, but some players focus more on one than the other. Midfielders see a lot of action during a game and usually run more than other positions. They must be good at transitioning the ball, quickly switching from defense to offense or offense to defense. They also help control the flow of the game and set up plays for their team. Midfield positions can include: center midfielder, wide midfielders, attacking midfielders, defensive midfielders.

Defenders—Defenders usually stay on the side of the field with their team's goal, and they work to keep the other team from scoring. They do this by stopping shots and breaking up the opponent's attacks. These players must be powerful and aggressive. Defensive positions can include: center back, fullbacks, wingbacks, sweeper.

Goalkeeper—The main job of the goalkeeper, or goalie, is to stop the ball from going into the net. They are the only player who can use their hands to control the ball, but only when they're in an area called the penalty box.

GLOSSARY

breakaway (BRAY-kuh-way)—when a player who has the ball gets past the other team's defense and rushes toward the goal

championship (CHAM-pee-uhn-ship)—a contest held to find out which team is the best at a sport

confident (KON-fi-duhnt)—having the belief that you can do something well

coverage (KUHV-rij)—newspaper articles and information given about a certain event or topic

embarrass (em-BAR-uhss)—to cause someone or yourself to feel silly and uncomfortable, usually in front of others

exhausting (ig-ZAW-sting)—very tiring

header (HED-ur)—a shot or pass made by hitting the ball on your head

interview (IN-tur-vyoo)—to ask questions and talk with someone to find out more about something; also, a meeting in which people talk to each other to get information

sensation (sen-SAY-shuhn)—something that lots of people are excited about and interested in

streak (STREEK)—a period of time when you are always doing very well or very poorly

transfer (TRANS-fer)—to move to a different place; also, someone who has changed schools

viral (VAHY-ruhl)—spreading very quickly from being shared by many people on the internet

ABOUT THE AUTHOR

Brandon Terrell is the author of numerous children's books, including several volumes in both the Tony Hawk 900 Revolution series and the Tony Hawk Live2Skate series. He has also written several Spine Shivers titles and is the author of the *Sports Illustrated Kids*: Time Machine Magazine series. When not hunched over his laptop, Brandon enjoys watching movies and TV, reading, watching and playing baseball, and spending time with his wife and two children at his home in Minnesota.

ABOUT THE ARTISTS

Mel Joy San Juan started creating manga-style comics as a teenager. After joining Glass House Graphics Asia, Mel Joy expanded into the U.S. market. Before long, she was drawing Dark-Hunters with best-selling author Sherrilyn Kenyon, as well as such varied projects as Call of Duty, Spider-Man, Knightingail, and concept design and storyboard work on several feature films. She resides in Cavite, Philippines.

Jaymes Reed has operated the company Digital-CAPS: Comic Book Lettering since 2003. He has done lettering for many publishers, most notably Avatar Press. He's also the only letterer working with Inception Strategies, an Aboriginal-Australian publisher that develops social comics with public service messages for the Australian government. Jaymes is a 2012 and 2013 Shel Dorf Award Nominee.

Berenice Muñiz is a graphic designer and illustrator from Monterrey, Mexico. She has done work for publicity agencies, art exhibitions, and even created her own webcomic. These days, Berenice is devoted to illustrating comics as part of the Graphikslava crew.

READ THEM ALL!

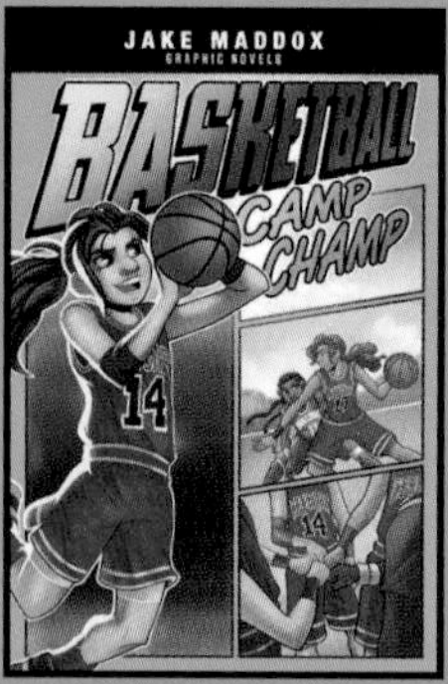
JAKE MADDOX
GRAPHIC NOVELS
BASKETBALL CAMP CHAMP

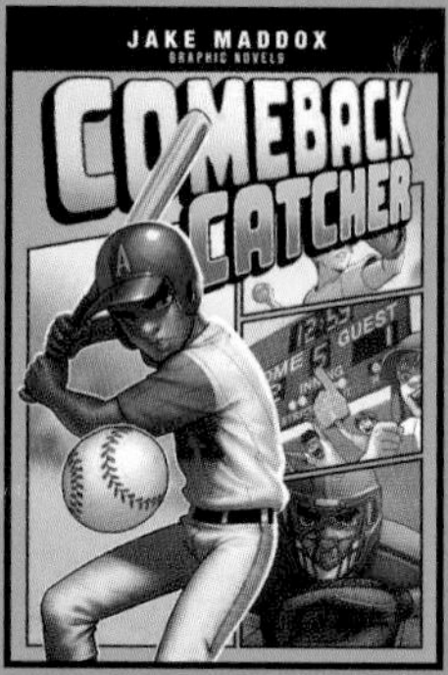
JAKE MADDOX
GRAPHIC NOVELS
COMEBACK CATCHER

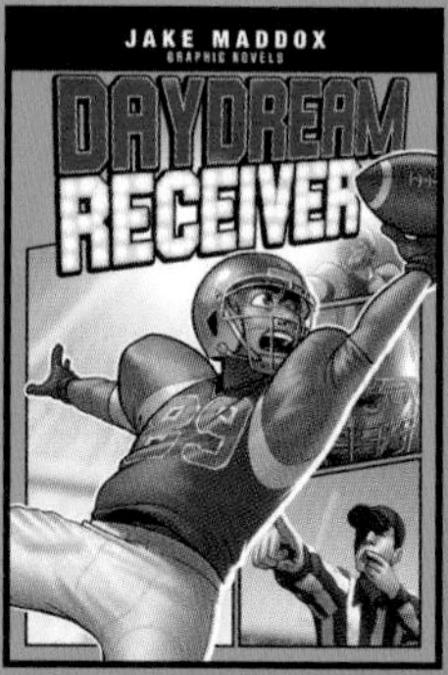
JAKE MADDOX
GRAPHIC NOVELS
DAYDREAM RECEIVER

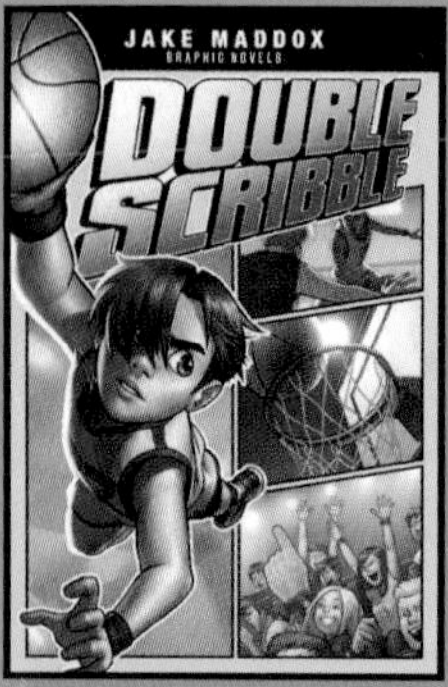
JAKE MADDOX
GRAPHIC NOVELS
DOUBLE DRIBBLE

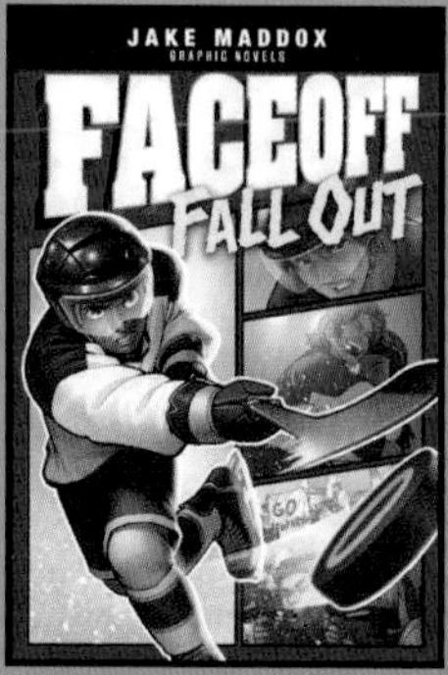
JAKE MADDOX
GRAPHIC NOVELS
FACEOFF FALL OUT

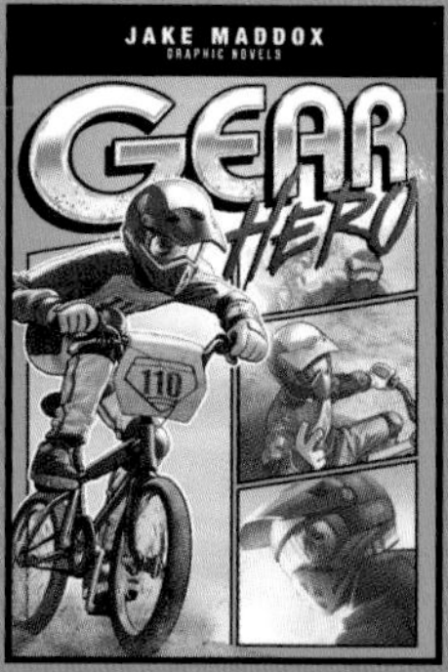
JAKE MADDOX
GRAPHIC NOVELS
GEAR HERO
110

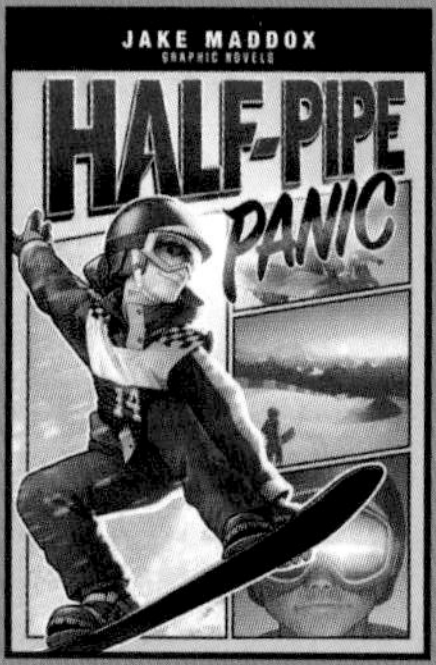
JAKE MADDOX
GRAPHIC NOVELS
HALF-PIPE PANIC

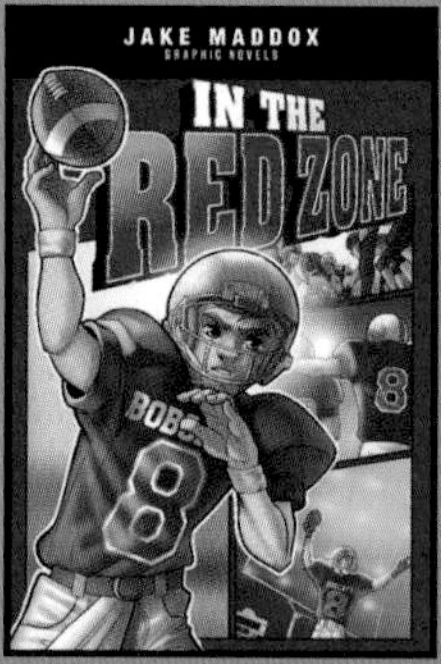
JAKE MADDOX
GRAPHIC NOVELS
IN THE RED ZONE

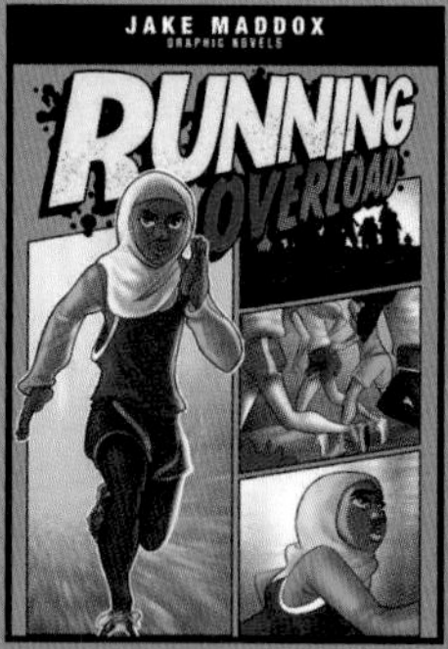
JAKE MADDOX
GRAPHIC NOVELS
RUNNING OVERLOAD

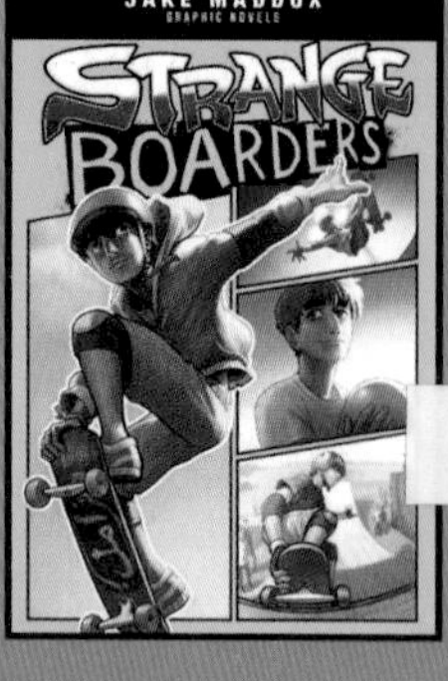
JAKE MADDOX
GRAPHIC NOVELS
STRANGE BOARDERS

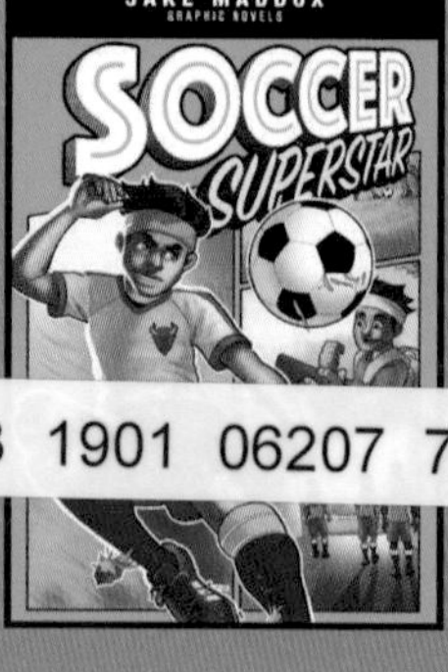
JAKE MADDOX
GRAPHIC NOVELS
SOCCER SUPERSTAR

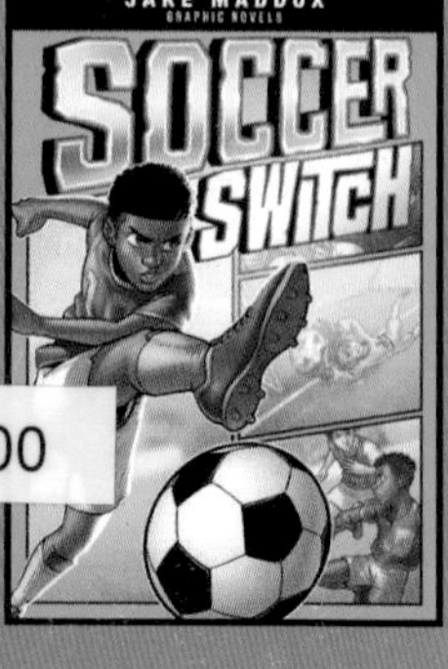
JAKE MADDOX
GRAPHIC NOVELS
SOCCER SWITCH